"She hates me."

"I would never do anything to hurt you," she said softly to the mare, trying to soothe her. Stardust flicked her ears, keeping an eye on Ashleigh, who reached slowly for the lead rope, a little less sure of her ability to handle the horse. This time Stardust appeared less flighty. Her head came down and she gave a long, deep snort, as if she'd been holding her breath.

Mrs. Griffen released her hold on the mare. "Walk her off, Ashleigh," she said. "I'll stay right beside you for a while." The mare seemed unwilling to follow, but finally she obeyed the tug on her lead rope and followed Ashleigh. Once the horse seemed to accept Ashleigh's control of the lead rope, Mrs. Griffen walked over to Ashleigh's father. Together they watched Ashleigh lead the mare in circles.

Every time she glanced at the mare, Stardust pulled away and pinned her ears. "What's wrong with her?" Ashleigh turned to her parents. "She hates me."

Collect all the books in the
Ashleigh series:

Coming soon:

ASHLEIGH'S Thoroughbred Collection

THOROUGHBRED

Ashleigh

WAITING FOR STARDUST

JOANNA CAMPBELL

HarperEntertainment
A Division of HarperCollinsPublishers

HarperEntertainment
A Division of HarperCollins*Publishers*
10 East 53rd Street, New York, NY 10022-5299

This is a work of fiction. The characters, incidents, and
dialogues are products of the author's imagination and are not to be
construed as real. Any resemblance to actual events or persons,
living or dead, is entirely coincidental.

Produced by 17th Street Productions,
a division of Daniel Weiss Associates, Inc.

HarperCollins books are available at special quantity
discounts for bulk purchases for sales promotions, premiums, or
fund-raising. For information please write:
Special Markets Department, HarperCollins Publishers Inc.,
10 East 53rd Street, New York, NY 10022-5299.

ISBN 0-06-106544-7

HarperCollins®, ■®, and HarperEntertainment™ are trademarks of
HarperCollins Publishers Inc.

Cover art © 1999 by Daniel Weiss Associates, Inc.

First printing: February 1999

Printed in the United States of America

Visit HarperEntertainment on the World Wide Web at
http://www.harpercollins.com

❖ 10 9 8 7 6 5 4 3 2 1

The author wishes to thank Mary Newhall Anderson for her help in writing this book.

1

"Ouch, Rory, you just ran over my foot again!" Ashleigh Griffen looked over the top of her new horse book at her five-year-old brother. His blond head was bent over the bright yellow dump truck as he ran it back and forth on the living room carpet. Ashleigh smiled wearily.

"Why don't you take your truck outside?" she suggested.

"Can't." Rory growled like a truck engine, then drove his new toy into the coffee table. "Mom said dinner will be ready pretty soon. I don't want to miss Christmas dessert."

Ashleigh rolled her eyes and sighed good-naturedly. "Whatever," she said, turning back to her book.

In one corner of the room, the Griffens' Christmas tree stood tall and green, decorated with a twinkling display of colored lights and bright ornaments. Most of the decorations had horse themes. Even the brood-mares who lived at Edgardale, the Griffens' Thorough-bred breeding farm, had their own ornaments hung on the tree. The black, bay, and white horse figurines dangled from the pine tree's branches, prancing in the air.

The floor had become Rory's construction zone, and he busily pushed balled-up wrapping paper with his new bulldozer, making a pile to put in the back of his dump truck.

"You're going to wear those trucks out before Christmas day is even over," Ashleigh said. She closed her book and watched her brother maneuver his truck around the room.

"Am not." Rory sat on his heels and folded his arms across his chest. "If you weren't sitting on the floor, your feet wouldn't be in the way."

Ashleigh sighed and tucked her feet under her, pushing a strand of long dark hair behind her ear. "You don't have to drive right where I'm sitting."

Rory ignored her. "Put Prince Charming in the back of the truck. I'll take him for a ride."

Ashleigh set aside her book and quickly put a pro-tective hand on her favorite Christmas gift, a Maine coon kitten. The tiny cat was curled by her side, purring. "No way," Ashleigh said, petting the tiger-striped ball of fur. His long brown and gray coat felt feathery soft under her hand. "I've seen the way you drive, Rory."

Ashleigh's thirteen-year-old sister, Caroline, sat on the sofa, her bare toes sticking up in the air. "Do you like my new polish?" Caroline smoothed her blond hair with the palm of her hand, keeping her freshly polished fingernails from getting smudged.

Ashleigh barely glanced at her sister. "It looks fine."

"You didn't even look. The bright pink matches my new mohair sweater. This is such a great Christmas," Caroline sighed. "I got everything I wanted."

Ashleigh shrugged and picked up her new riding helmet. "Me too," she said, although she didn't really mean it. Ashleigh certainly hadn't gotten what she wanted most: a horse of her own. Instead, she'd given away the horse she could've had.

Only a few days before, Ashleigh had made the most difficult decision she'd ever faced in all her ten years— to give up Lightning, the white mare she'd rescued from abuse, brought back to health, and loved with all her heart. She'd given the mare as a Christmas gift to the children at the Hopewell Center, a cancer treatment center for kids. She knew Lightning would be showered with love and would bring a lot of happiness to Hopewell, but she missed the mare so much it hurt.

3

For months, while she had nursed Lightning back to health, she'd dreamed that Lightning would be hers one day, that the humane society, which had authority over the rescued mare, would let the Griffens adopt her. But the humane society had another home in mind, the Hopewell Center, and in the end it was left to Ashleigh to make the final decision.

"Paint my toes," Rory said, scrambling to his feet and heading for Caroline. "Do you have tractor green?"

"Boys don't wear polish," Caroline said, quickly moving her manicure supplies out of her brother's reach.

Rory turned away promptly. "Then take me to the barn, Ash."

Ashleigh smiled at how easily her little brother was distracted.

"You promised you'd help me ride Moe," he added.

"Good idea, Ashleigh," Mrs. Griffen said from the kitchen doorway, her own blond hair pulled back from her face in a ponytail, a bright green and red plaid apron covering her clothes. Rory and Caroline took after their mother, while Ashleigh looked more like their dark-haired father. "Dinner won't be ready for another hour or so, so you two have time to take Moe out for a little while."

Ashleigh popped her new riding helmet on her

head and rose to her feet. "Okay, Rory. Let's go."

After being in the warm, Christmassy-smelling house, the air felt crisp and cold and smelled of winter. The ground was dry and hard. There had been no snow at Edgardale this Christmas day. Ashleigh took her little brother's hand, and they hurried down to the big barn. Just inside the door, Ashleigh could hear the soft rustle of bedding and the sound of horses eating. She took a deep breath, filling her lungs with the wonderful smell of a barn full of horses. They started down the row of stalls, where the ten broodmares, their foals, and Moe, a Shetland pony, were eating their own Christmas dinner.

Wanderer, the farm's best broodmare, stuck her head over the half door of her stall and whinnied, demanding Ashleigh's attention. Ashleigh rubbed the black mare's velvety nose. "I'll bring Prince Charming down to the barn tomorrow morning so you can meet him," she said to the mare. The soft munching sound of the horses eating their hay filled the air. When they passed a particular empty stall, Ashleigh closed her eyes for a moment and pretended Lightning was still there. She imagined herself walking up to the mare's stall and giving her long white nose a kiss.

But Lightning was with the children at Hopewell, and pretending wasn't going to bring her back.

Ashleigh quickly opened her eyes and moved past the empty stall.

She and Rory made their way down the aisle, stroking the soft noses of the mares and foals as they approached Moe's stall. Thick-coated Moe was the one animal in the barn that didn't need a blanket to keep him warm during the cold winter nights. Each of the delicate Thoroughbreds had a heavy winter blanket, which they wore much of the time.

Ashleigh led the pony from his stall. "If you want to ride," she told Rory, "you have to help groom."

While Ashleigh clipped the crossties to Moe's halter, Rory found a brush and began stroking it along the little molasses-colored pony's shaggy coat. "How come he's so hairy?" he asked. "The other horses are nice and smooth."

"Because they're Thoroughbreds and he's a pony, that's why."

"Oh."

The answer seemed to satisfy Rory. Ashleigh quickly saddled Moe and led him outside. "I'll ride first," she said.

"Why don't you ride someone else?" Rory demanded. "I want to ride Moe. He's my pony now."

"We have to share him," Ashleigh explained, wishing she could just let her little brother have Moe to himself. "I don't have Lightning anymore, and we can't ride the broodmares." Only their parents did that, and only when their foals were big enough to get left behind. But Ashleigh wasn't allowed to ride the Thoroughbreds. *At least not yet,* she thought. It was her dream to become a jockey.

"I'm littlest, so I should go first," Rory said.

"I'll just warm him up for you." Before Rory could protest again, Ashleigh swung onto Moe's back. She missed climbing onto Lightning's back, having the feel of a real horse under her. Moe's short legs made his walk choppy, and when Ashleigh moved him into a trot, she could only remember the feel of riding Lightning with her long, smooth strides. But Lightning wasn't hers to ride anymore.

She tried not to think about the beautiful white mare, but with every jolting step Moe took, she regretted more and more her decision to give up the horse she had helped rescue.

"My turn," Rory yelled. Ashleigh reined the pony to a stop. She had almost forgotten about Rory. Reluctant to end her ride, even if it was just on old Moe, she took him around the paddock for one more turn, pushing him into a canter. "I wish I had a real horse," she murmured as the pony's short legs churned under him, covering very little ground for all the work he was doing.

"Now," Rory yelled, stamping his feet. "You're too big for him anyway, Ashleigh. And you've been on him for hours!"

"I have not," Ashleigh protested, but she stopped the pony and hopped off. She helped her little brother into the saddle, then adjusted the stirrups for his shorter legs.

"Now remember," she told him, "don't pull on his mouth. You just need a little contact with the reins."

"I know, Ashleigh. I know how to ride my own pony." Rory walked off, sitting straight on Moe's back.

Ashleigh watched him for several minutes. Rory looked perfect on Moe. And he was right. She was too big for the pony.

"Time to go in," she said after a while. They put Moe away, taking the time to groom him well before they trudged back to the house.

The lights from the farmhouse windows glowed golden in the gathering dusk. When Ashleigh opened the kitchen door, a gust of warm air enveloped her, filling her senses with the wonderful smells of her mother's clove-studded ham, pecan pie, and all the other sweet, spicy treats of Christmas. *If barns smell the very best,* she thought, *a house at Christmas is almost as good.*

"Mona called while you were out," Mrs. Griffen

said when they walked into the kitchen. "She sounded pretty excited."

"Thanks, Mom." Ashleigh picked up the phone and dialed her best friend's number.

Mona Gardener answered the phone on the first ring. "Ash, you have to come over! I got her! I got my horse!"

Ashleigh sucked in her breath, then answered in her cheeriest voice. "That's great, Mona. Did you name her Frisky, like we talked about?"

"Just like Frisky Mister, the racehorse, and the best part is she's a registered Thoroughbred, too!"

Ashleigh couldn't hold back a twinge of jealousy, remembering how she and Mona had talked about getting horses for Christmas. Only she'd made the choice to let Lightning go to the kids at Hopewell. But that wasn't Mona's fault. "How big is she? What color?" Ashleigh asked, her curiosity getting the better of her.

Mona giggled. "About sixteen hands, and she's a light bay with four white stockings. She's so awesome, Ash. You have to come over and see her."

"Have you ridden her yet?" Ashleigh thought of her own short ride on Moe and felt her shoulders slump. She should be happy that Mona had her own horse, but it just wasn't fair.

"I've already tried her in the paddock. She's really gentle and kind, like Silver, only riding her is way better than riding a Welsh pony. She's already had some training over jumps, too. I can do so much more now!"

Ashleigh listened in silence, pressing her head against the cold pane of the kitchen window, trying to remember to be happy for Mona.

"Ash?" Mona's voice dropped. "I'm sorry. I'm not trying to rub it in that I have a horse."

"I know." Ashleigh felt bad that she couldn't sound more excited for Mona's sake. "It's not your fault. I'm really glad for you."

"I wish you'd kept Lightning."

Ashleigh swallowed around a lump in her throat. "The kids at Hopewell will love her as much as I do, Mona. Mom and Dad said the best gift you can give someone is one you'd like for yourself. I guess I gave the best gift ever, didn't I?"

There was a moment of silence on both ends, and Ashleigh fought to keep from crying.

"I want you to come over and ride Frisky," Mona said quickly. "You just have to try her out. It'll be fun to see how she moves with someone else in the saddle. Maybe you can come over tomorrow, since it's getting dark now."

Ashleigh's spirits lifted at the thought of riding Mona's new Thoroughbred.

"I can't wait," she said. And she meant it.

Ashleigh told Mona all about her new kitten, Prince Charming, before Mr. Griffen called everyone for Christmas dinner and she had to hang up.

"I got a call from Sally, the physical therapist at Hopewell," Mrs. Griffen said, handing a dish mounded with mashed potatoes to her husband.

Ashleigh sat up straight, gripping the edges of her chair with her hands. Maybe Lightning wasn't working out at Hopewell and could come back to Edgardale after all. Ashleigh knew it was a selfish thought, though.

"Is Lightning okay?" she asked, letting go of the chair to take the bowl of fruit salad Caroline held out.

Mrs. Griffen smiled. "More than fine, Ashleigh. Sally says she's happy as can be. And Sally would know. She's very experienced with horses. Lightning has lots of good company in the barn, even when the kids aren't out there petting and brushing her."

Ashleigh knew Lightning wasn't lonely. Hopewell was nothing like the home Ashleigh and Mona had helped rescue her from, where she had been starved and beaten and left alone for days at a time. At Hopewell she had Ollie, the potbellied pig; the chickens, Daisy and Pumpkin; the black and white goat, Barney; and of course Mortimer, the duck who acted like a watchdog, quacking loudly and flapping his wings at any new visitor to the barn.

"Maybe after dinner you could call Kira, Ashleigh." Mr. Griffen handed her a plate laden with a fragrant slice of ham.

Kira was a patient at the Hopewell Center. She and Ashleigh had become friends when Ashleigh had made the decision to give Lightning to Hopewell. Kira loved horses, too, and was thrilled to have Lightning. Kira and Ashleigh were the same age, but Kira seemed much older somehow. Kira explained to Ashleigh that having cancer had made her see things a lot differently. Ashleigh admired the way Kira didn't let her illness get her down. Kira was determined that one day she would be stronger and could start riding lessons again. In the meantime, she spent as much time with Lightning as she could.

Ashleigh knew Prince Charming had been part of her parents' way of helping ease the sadness of letting Lightning go to the center. Ashleigh loved the fluffy little kitten, but in her heart she wasn't ready to let Lightning go. Not yet.

After dinner she helped Caroline clean the kitchen, then picked up the phone to call Kira at Hopewell.

"Merry Christmas," Kira said in a cheerful voice when she came to the phone.

"Merry Christmas," Ashleigh responded, even though the first words that almost came out of her mouth were to ask how Lightning was.

"My parents came down for the day," Kira said. "I got so many presents. They don't have to go back to Ohio until tomorrow night, so we have lots of time together."

Ashleigh could hear a wistful tone in the other girl's voice. She thought of her own parents in the other room. She couldn't even imagine being so far away from them for months at a time. "You're really brave, Kira."

The other girl sighed. "No, I'm not. It's just that I don't have a choice. I have to do whatever it takes to get better. I am going to get well and go home. Soon."

Suddenly Ashleigh felt spoiled and selfish for even considering that Lightning might come back to Edgardale. "I'm so glad you have Lightning there to keep you company," she said, realizing she meant it with all her heart.

When Kira spoke again, her voice sounded more cheerful. "Me too," she said. "You're the brave one, Ash. You gave up the most wonderful horse in the world so that she could be here with me."

When she hung up, Ashleigh felt better about Lightning than she had in days. She headed for the barn with Prince Charming tucked in her jacket. The warm bundle of fluff purred against her shoulder, content to be snuggled close.

Ashleigh stopped in front of Moe's stall and opened her jacket so that Prince Charming could see out. Moe sniffed at the little creature, and the kitten batted his tiny paw at Moe's nose. Moe bobbed his head and whuffed softly.

"Why am I not surprised to see you down here on Christmas night?"

Ashleigh glanced up to see Kurt Bradley, the Griffens' stable hand, walking down the aisle. Kurt had lost his ten-year-old daughter to leukemia a year before he started working at Edgardale, and now he volunteered at Hopewell. He had taken a keen interest in Lightning, too. It was Kurt who had brought the mare to Edgardale and helped Ashleigh nurse her back to health.

"Merry Christmas," she said in greeting.

"Merry Christmas, Ashleigh." Kurt stopped beside her and smiled down at Moe and Prince Charming. "It looks like Moe and your new stuffed toy like each other."

Ashleigh ran her hand down Prince Charming's

back. "He isn't a toy," she replied with a grin, holding up the kitten so Kurt could hear him purring. "He's my Christmas present."

"Looks like he's going to be huge," Kurt said, rubbing his finger beneath the kitten's chin. "This barn needs some big cats to keep the mice out of the feed."

"But he's not going to live in the barn," Ashleigh said, stroking Prince Charming's soft fur. "He's going to sleep with me. Aren't you?" She glanced at Kurt's slacks and sports shirt, clothes he wore only for special occasions. "Did you go to Hopewell for Christmas dinner?"

Kurt nodded. "We had a great time. Some of the kids' parents couldn't make it today, so it was nice to be there to kind of fill in. I checked on Lightning for you. She's overdosing on carrots, but she looks just fine."

Ashleigh pressed her lips together and tried to keep smiling.

"You did a great thing letting her go there, Ashleigh. I know it was tough for you, but she's good therapy for the kids. They adore her, and she seems to like all the love and attention."

A few tears crowded at the corners of Ashleigh's eyes. She hugged Prince Charming to her face, using him to hide behind. "I'm glad," she murmured. "Merry Christmas, Kurt."

"Merry Christmas," he said, and headed for his apartment over the barn.

Ashleigh wandered back up to the house. It was better to give than to receive, she reminded herself. She thought of the happiness in Kira's voice when she talked about Lightning, and how everyone told her what a good thing she'd done. Still, Ashleigh didn't feel any better. As much as she tried to tell herself that helping others should be enough, it still hurt to think that giving Lightning to Hopewell meant she had given up the one thing she wanted more than anything in the world—a horse.

Prince Charming batted at her chin, and Ashleigh hugged him close. "I know I still have you. But now Mona has Frisky and I don't have a horse at all."

She sighed and looked up at the inky black sky. Stars sparkled and glimmered overhead, but one star seemed to glisten brighter than the others.

"Starlight, star bright," Ashleigh whispered, looking at the big, sparkling star. "Biggest star I see tonight. I wish I may, I wish I might, have the wish I wish tonight." She took a deep breath, closed her eyes, and concentrated. "I wish," she said out loud, "for my own horse."

2

Ashleigh hurried down to the barn after breakfast, grateful for her riding gloves and warm jacket. The sun reflected brightly on the white fences but didn't warm things up at all. A light frost glittered on Edgardale's rolling pastures and sparkled on the roof of the barn. A perfect winter vacation day, Ashleigh decided, puffing out misty clouds with each breath.

Ashleigh gathered Moe's tack and began to get him ready for the ride over to Mona's. When she bent way down to reach Moe's girth, she was struck by how small he was. She tried not to think about it. At least she could ride. That was what was important, not that she was only riding little Moe.

Ashleigh loved Moe. They'd spent so many happy hours together and had some wonderful adventures, but she needed a bigger horse. She would be riding over to see Mona's new Thoroughbred on a pony she

17

was rapidly outgrowing. But she'd made the decision to give Lightning to the center, so there was no one to blame but herself.

Rory came rushing into the barn as Ashleigh finished tacking up Moe. "Where are you going with Moe?" he cried. Ashleigh sighed. How many times would she have to explain the situation to her little brother? Moe had become Rory's pony when Ashleigh had advanced to Lightning, and neither Ashleigh nor Rory had expected that Ashleigh would ever have to ride Moe again.

"I'm riding over to Mona's to see her new horse," Ashleigh explained. "Don't worry, I won't be too long."

"But he's my pony now," Rory protested. "You're too big to ride him anymore!"

"I know, Rory, but I don't have any other horse to ride, and it won't hurt him if I ride him over to Mona's. It's not exactly a long way away."

Rory scowled. "You'd better not hurt him."

"I'd never hurt Moe, Rory, and you know it," Ashleigh shot back. Then she led Moe outside and mounted up. As she headed out she knew Rory was scowling after her. Ashleigh understood her little brother's frustration, but it wasn't her fault she didn't have another horse to ride. It was Moe or nothing.

Ashleigh trotted Moe along the grassy verge of the

road to Mona's place, which neighbored theirs. The frozen grass crunched under Moe's hooves. Ashleigh inhaled deeply as she rode along, filling her lungs with cold, sharp air.

Mona's parents weren't horse breeders like the Griffens. They owned about ten acres, a farmhouse, and a big barn that had once been part of a larger property. Mona's father was a lawyer, and her mother worked in town during the day. But Mona's mother loved horses and rode and sometimes competed in local shows. She had her own horse and had gotten Mona a Welsh pony named Silver when Mona had first shown an interest in riding.

Ashleigh reined Moe into Mona's drive along the white rail fence, beside a large pasture. Mrs. Gardener's big chestnut hunter was grazing in the pasture with Silver, Mona's pony.

When Moe spotted Silver, he whinnied to his old friend. The whinny felt as though it started at his tail and passed all the way to his nose. Ashleigh laughed as Silver raised his head and called back. She petted Moe's furry neck. "You're such a nice little pony," Ashleigh said. "Rory's right. I am too big for you. But without a horse of my own, it's you or nothing." Ashleigh slumped in the saddle. She could only hope it wouldn't be this way forever.

Ashleigh waved at Mr. Gardener, who was standing on the wide porch of their gray house, checking the bulbs on their Christmas lights. Patches of sparkly frost glittered where the sunlight touched them.

She headed Moe toward the red barn. The Gardeners didn't need a lot of space for their three pleasure horses, so Mr. Gardener had converted half the barn into a garage. On the other side were several stalls and the hayloft.

Mona stood outside the barn waiting for Ashleigh, her hard hat dangling from her fingers. Like Ashleigh, she was bundled in a heavy jacket and riding gloves. Mona and Ashleigh looked enough alike to be sisters, but Mona kept her dark hair cut short. Mona's cheeks were bright pink in the cold weather, and her gray eyes sparkled with excitement. Ashleigh waved and steered Moe toward her.

"She's inside. Come on!" Mona called.

As Ashleigh approached on Moe, Mona danced in front of the barn, jumping from one foot to the other, her breath making frosty clouds around her head. Then she darted into the barn. Ashleigh hopped from Moe's back and led him into an empty stall. She slipped his bridle off, then followed Mona, who had hurried to the other end of the barn.

Ashleigh stopped in the middle of the aisle. Her

breath caught when she saw the beautiful bay mare Mona led out of the last stall.

"She's gorgeous," Ashleigh cried. Frisky looked fit and had the conformation of a racehorse. In comparison to the Edgardale broodmares, with their wide, heavy bellies, Frisky looked lean and elegant. Mona stood by her new horse's head, holding the lead line, a proud look on her face. Ashleigh envied her best friend so much it ached.

Then Frisky arched her neck and sniffed in Ashleigh's direction. "She smells Moe," Ashleigh said, admiring the graceful mare. Frisky raised her head and released a loud whinny. Moe answered with a shrill pony call. The girls laughed, and Ashleigh shoved her jealousy aside. Mona deserved a nice horse.

"She's sweet, too," Mona said, giving her new mare a loving look. "Come and meet her."

Ashleigh walked up slowly, standing to the side so that Frisky could sniff her shoulder. She raised her hand and let Frisky lower her nose to snuffle her palm.

"Hi, Frisky," she said in a quiet voice. "I'm Ashleigh, Mona's best friend. Except for you, of course." She and Mona giggled. Frisky nudged Ashleigh's arm, and Ashleigh reached up to rub the whorl between the mare's large, dark eyes. "You are beautiful." Ashleigh inhaled the wonderful perfume of horse and smiled at Mona. "You're so lucky."

"I know." Mona beamed. "I never dreamed my parents would get me such a great horse."

"She looks like she must have been bred to race," Ashleigh said, stepping back to look at Frisky's muscular shoulders and long legs.

Mona nodded. "She ran a few races, but she never won anything. She placed a couple of seconds and thirds. I guess she wasn't interested in going really fast, which is fine by me."

Ashleigh slid her hand along Frisky's smooth, dark flank. "So they bought her right off the track?" Frisky didn't seem to radiate the tension Ashleigh thought all racehorses had. The horses she saw at the track almost hummed with nervous energy. Frisky seemed much calmer and more easygoing.

"The people my parents bought her from weren't the ones who raced her," Mona said. "They bought her at auction as a jumping prospect and put several months into retraining her."

"Why didn't they keep her?" Ashleigh asked. "She has great conformation and nice flat knees. She'd be an excellent jumper."

Mona nodded. "They bought a Dutch warmblood,

too, and decided he was better for the kind of jumping they want to do."

"So she goes really well, huh?" Ashleigh kept her hand on Frisky's long, sleek neck. She felt another stab of envy for her friend. Why couldn't her own mom and dad have found a horse like Frisky for her?

"Her trot—" Mona started to say.

"Is nothing like Silver's, right?" Ashleigh thought of her own bouncing ride on Moe.

"No kidding," Mona said. "She's got nice long strides, not like those short-legged ponies."

Ashleigh felt her sense of humor fade.

"Sorry," Mona said, looking down. "The ponies are still great. We've had so much fun on them, right? I mean, if it weren't for Moe and Silver, we never would have found Lightning. We never could have followed those narrow deer trails in the woods on big horses."

Ashleigh forced herself to smile. "I know," she said wistfully, thinking again of Lightning. "And if I'd marked our trail better, we never would have gotten so lost. That was the scariest ride of my life. But it turned out all right, because we got Lightning away from that awful man."

Mona nodded her agreement. "Do you want to try Frisky now?"

"You bet!" Ashleigh said. "You'd think living on a

breeding farm, I'd ride Thoroughbreds all the time, but I've never even sat on one before. Now with Lightning gone, there's only Moe to ride again."

"Well, you can ride Frisky, too," Mona said as she led her new horse to the crossties. "It'll just take a minute to tack her up."

"Great!" Ashleigh felt a rush of excitement at the prospect of finally riding a Thoroughbred. And even better, one that had actually run in races.

Once Frisky was saddled, the girls led her to a small paddock near the barn. Mona gave Ashleigh a leg up. For a minute Ashleigh sat on the mare's tall back, reveling in the idea that she was sitting on a racehorse. Finally she adjusted the stirrups, resisting the urge to shorten them enough to make her feel like a jockey.

She asked Frisky for a walk. Ashleigh felt so comfortable on the attentive, obedient mare that in a minute she urged Frisky into a trot. With Frisky's long, fluid strides, so different from Moe's spine-slamming little steps, Ashleigh found she could easily sit the trot. In fact, Ashleigh had to admit that Frisky's smooth trot was even better than Lightning's.

When she asked the mare to canter, Frisky moved into an easy, rocking gait that made Ashleigh feel as if she were sailing over waves on the ocean. Even though they were in the small paddock, Frisky tried to increase her speed and move into a gallop. Ashleigh wished they were on a nice grassy lane. She'd crouch over the powerful horse's shoulders like a real jockey and see how fast they could go.

Riding Frisky was heavenly. She never wanted to stop. Frisky didn't want to stop, either. Ashleigh had to rein her in small circles to slow her down. Frisky still hadn't forgotten her racetrack past.

Ashleigh stopped the mare in front of Mona and sighed. "She's great. I love riding her." She stroked the mare's smooth neck. "You are so lucky."

"I want to take her up to the pasture," Mona said, "but Mom said I can't go alone until I know her better, and Mom hasn't had time to go. Can you and Moe ride up there with us?"

"Moe could never keep up with Frisky," Ashleigh said, sliding from the mare's back. It was a long way down. Back on the ground, Ashleigh's good mood deflated fast and her jealousy returned. Mona knew that Moe was no match for a Thoroughbred. "I'm sure your parents will let you go out on your own in a few days," she added impatiently.

"I know," Mona said, "but I really want to try her up there now. Come with me, please, Ash?" Mona pressed her palms together and gave Ashleigh a pleading look.

Ashleigh rolled her eyes. "Okay, but no races. Moe could never keep up."

"I know that," Mona said. "I don't want to race. I just want to ride Frisky outside the ring and see how we do."

Ashleigh headed back to the barn for Moe. In minutes the two girls were mounted and ready to go.

Ashleigh felt a jolt of envy as she saw how good Mona looked up on Frisky. Beside them on Moe, Ashleigh noticed that her head only came up to Mona's waist. Mona looked like a real rider, and Ashleigh felt childish and dumpy. She tried not to let it bother her as they set off over the large pasture behind the Gardeners' barn.

The Gardeners' horses didn't graze that part of the field much, so the pasture was rough. In some areas the grasses were cropped low and the weeds stood tall. The horses picked their way up the hilly pasture.

"This way," Mona said, nudging Frisky into a trot. Ashleigh posted to Moe's jouncy gait and followed Frisky up a steep hill. Mona and Frisky reached the top of the hill quickly thanks to Frisky's smooth, long strides. She turned the mare and waited for Ashleigh and Moe.

"I told you we couldn't keep up," Ashleigh complained when they finally reached the top.

"It wasn't a race," Mona protested. "The pasture is

pretty smooth here. I'm going to try cantering her."

Ashleigh watched as Mona cantered off and reined Frisky in a wide circle. The mare moved effortlessly, seeming not the least bit tired, while Moe had broken into a sweat despite the cold temperature. Ashleigh kept him walking so that he wouldn't get chilled.

"How did we look?" Mona called to her a few minutes later when she slowed Frisky to a trot.

"Perfect," Ashleigh answered, unable to keep the envy out of her voice. Mona had to know how good she looked on that beautiful mare. She didn't need to ask Ashleigh, and she didn't need a cheering section. "I'm going to head back," Ashleigh said. "I promised Rory I'd bring Moe back before too long."

Ashleigh turned the pony and started down the hill. If there was one advantage Moe had, it was his surefootedness. He'd be able to travel downhill over the rough ground faster than long-legged Frisky.

"Wait, Ash," Mona called.

"Race you!" Ashleigh called over her shoulder. She calculated the shortest route to the pasture gate, then heeled Moe forward. The pony willingly picked up his pace, and the two of them scrambled down the hill.

Ashleigh heard Frisky's hoofbeats behind them and urged Moe to speed up. Mona called after her, but Ashleigh ignored her friend. She couldn't stand having Mona show her up, even if it wasn't on purpose.

The need to win filled her mind. She headed Moe through a rough patch of weeds Mona had avoided earlier. Going straight through the weeds would take them directly to the gate. It was the fastest way. Ashleigh stood in the stirrups and glanced under her arm. Mona and Frisky were still pretty far behind

"We're going to win, Moe!" Ashleigh called, leaning forward on the pony's neck and urging him forward. "You can do it, boy!"

The words were barely out of her mouth when Moe suddenly went down to his knees, throwing Ashleigh over his head into the brush. She landed hard, face-down in the dried weed stalks. She lay there, stunned, for several seconds. She thought she could hear Mona calling her, but her ears were ringing loudly. Mona's voice sounded very far away. Ashleigh realized she hadn't taken a breath since she landed. She felt as if she'd been punched in the stomach.

"Ash! Ashleigh! Are you okay?"

Ashleigh rolled to her side, then slowly sat up, struggling to inhale after having the wind knocked out of her. Mona rushed over, leading Frisky.

"I was trying to tell you not to go this way," Mona said, her voice frightened and angry. "It's full of woodchuck holes."

Ashleigh shook her head, trying to clear her thoughts. Moe must have stepped in a hole. Was he all right? She looked over to where Moe had gone down and felt a rush of relief when she saw him on his feet.

Slowly Ashleigh stood and took a deep breath. She took a step toward the pony and stopped cold. Moe's knees were badly scraped, and he was holding his right foreleg off the ground. The pony's head drooped. Ashleigh felt her stomach drop and a sick lump rise to her throat.

"Oh, no!" She hurried to Moe's side, fighting back tears. "Moe, oh, poor Moe. What have I done?"

3

Moe gazed at her with trusting eyes, but Ashleigh knew she had betrayed him. She knelt and ran her hands down his injured leg. Moe stood still, his nose resting on her back. A trail of hot tears slid down her cheeks.

"Do you think it might be broken?" Mona asked in a hushed voice. Ashleigh glanced up. Mona's face was pale with worry.

"I don't know," Ashleigh said, wishing she could make time go backward. She would never run Moe like that again. "I hope not. But we need to get help."

"I'll get my mom," Mona said quickly. "You stay here with Moe. He's not the only one hurt, Ash—your face is pretty scratched up. It looks terrible." Mona swung onto Frisky's back and cantered toward the house. Ashleigh reached up to touch her face with her fingertips. It felt rough and sore. But she didn't care.

Moe's injured leg was foremost on her mind.

Ashleigh turned to the pony. "I'm so sorry, Moe. I can't believe I did this to you. I'm terrible." Moe rubbed his head against her chest, and Ashleigh felt a sob welling up from deep inside her. "I hurt you so badly, and you still love me. I don't deserve you, Moe." Tears streamed down her face as she cradled the pony's head. "This has to be a nightmare," she moaned. "I want to just wake up and make it go away."

"Ashleigh!" She looked down the hill and saw Mona's mother hurrying in her direction.

When she reached Ashleigh and Moe, Mrs. Gardener's eyes widened. "You're really scratched up," she said. "Are you hurt anywhere but your face?"

Ashleigh shook her head. "I'm fine," she said, although the side of her face felt stiff and funny, and the ringing in her ears still made everything else sound distant. "It's Moe. He has a broken leg."

Mrs. Gardener dropped to her knees and ran her hands along Moe's cannon bone. She glanced up at Ashleigh, frowning. "There's some heat," she said, "but I don't think it's broken. It could be just a pulled tendon."

Ashleigh felt a little better now that she knew Moe's leg probably wasn't broken.

"Mona's calling your parents." She dug into her jacket pocket, pulling out a rolled bandage and a leg wrap. "Hold the little guy while I wrap his leg. We need to keep it stable so that he doesn't injure it any worse. I told Mona to ask your parents to bring the trailer over so you can get Moe to Dr. Frankel's clinic."

Beginning at Moe's pastern, she carefully wound the padded cotton leg wrap around his leg to just below his knee. She covered that with a bandage, finishing with masking tape to hold it in place.

After she finished with Moe's leg, Mrs. Gardener turned to Ashleigh. "You're sure you didn't do anything more than scratch your face?"

"I'm sure," Ashleigh insisted.

"Why don't you wait at the house? Your face looks like it must hurt pretty bad." Mrs. Gardener looked worried, but Ashleigh shook her head.

"I'm not leaving Moe," she said, resting her hand on his muzzle.

It seemed to take forever before Ashleigh saw her parents' truck pulling into the drive, towing the two-horse trailer. Ashleigh's mother jumped from the pickup and ran across the field, Mr. Griffen at her heels.

"I'll stay with Moe," Mrs. Gardener said. "You go let your parents know you're okay."

Ashleigh didn't want to leave Moe. He was her responsibility. She started to open her mouth to argue, but one look at Mrs. Gardener's face stopped her.

She headed down the hill, dragging her feet. Her parents were going to skin her alive. And she deserved whatever punishment she got. She'd injured Moe by acting stupid, and her mom and dad were going to be furious. But when she reached her parents, their shocked faces stopped her. Her father placed his hands on her shoulders and looked hard at her face.

"You look like you took a nosedive into a briar patch," he said, frowning. "We need to get your face cleaned up. Are you hurt anywhere else?"

Ashleigh shrugged away from him. "I'm fine," she said, frustrated by the adults' concern over a few little scratches on her face. "It's Moe who's hurt." Fresh tears streaked down her face, stinging the cuts on her cheek.

She raised her hand to wipe away the tears and jerked her hand away when she brushed her face. It did hurt a lot more than she'd realized. But she deserved it. *Actually, I deserve worse,* she thought. *It should have been my leg that got hurt.*

Mrs. Griffen wrapped her arms around Ashleigh and gave her a comforting hug. "We'll take care of

Moe, sweetheart. Right now I need to be sure you're okay."

Ashleigh felt her mother's arm around her, but she knew she didn't deserve to be comforted. She was sure that after they saw what she'd done to Moe, her mom and dad were going to blow up.

"I'll take her to the house while you check the pony, Derek," Mrs. Griffen said.

Ashleigh started to protest that she should stay with Moe, but she closed her mouth and didn't say anything. She didn't want to see the look on her parents' faces after they finished examining Moe. Maybe when they got to the house she would wake up and find out this really was just a nightmare.

She let her mother lead her down the hill while her father hurried to where Mrs. Gardener waited with Moe.

When they got inside, the Gardeners' house felt too hot. Ashleigh hadn't realized how cold it was outside until she stepped into the kitchen.

"Let's get you cleaned up," her mother said, pressing Ashleigh onto a chair at the Gardeners' kitchen table. Mona brought her a pair of tweezers, and Ashleigh knew for sure she wasn't dreaming when her mother dabbed hydrogen peroxide on her skin.

"Ouch," she yelled, pulling her head away. The

warm air on her cold cheeks made them burn all by itself, and the medicine made it hurt a hundred times more.

"Hold still, sweetheart," her mother said in a no-nonsense voice. "We'll be done in a minute."

Ashleigh gritted her teeth and let her mother clean the scratches, pulling out any bits of dried weed that were embedded in her skin. It hurt like crazy, but she thought of Moe, standing on three legs in the pasture. Her face couldn't hurt any more than his leg. Poor Moe.

Mona stood near the kitchen sink, watching closely. Ashleigh ignored her friend. If Mona hadn't been showing off on Frisky, she thought angrily, she and Moe never would have fallen in the first place. But in her heart Ashleigh knew better. What she had done with Moe was her own fault. She couldn't blame Mona for wanting to ride her horse.

"We need to take you to the doctor," Mrs. Griffen said.

"I can't leave," Ashleigh said. "I have to hear what the vet says."

"I'll be here for Moe," Mona said. "I'll make sure he's okay, Ashleigh."

"Thanks, Mona," she murmured, wishing she could just melt into the floor.

"Thank you, Mona," Mrs. Griffen said. "Ashleigh, your father and Mona's mom are here, too. They'll make sure Moe is all right."

"But what if he has a broken leg?" Ashleigh began crying again. The tears made burning trails down her cheeks, but she didn't care how much her face hurt. "I can't leave him."

Mrs. Gardener stepped inside, bringing a gust of icy air with her. Ashleigh shivered, in spite of her warm jacket. "I need to call the vet. Derek is going to trailer Moe to the clinic."

"I'll ride with him!" Ashleigh jumped from her chair, sending it crashing to the floor.

Mrs. Griffen grabbed her arm. "Ashleigh, getting all worked up isn't going to help Moe. I need to get you to the doctor. Your father will take care of the pony."

"It's all right, Ashleigh," Mrs. Gardener said in a calm voice. "Your father thinks it's probably a pulled tendon, like I said. Moe is going to be fine. But the vet needs to see him."

"Can I borrow your car?" Mrs. Griffen asked Mona's mother. "Derek will need the truck and trailer to move Moe, and I want to get Ashleigh to the emergency room to have a doctor look her over."

Mrs. Gardener handed her the keys, and Ashleigh silently followed her mother outside.

"Moe's in good hands, Ash," her mother said, opening the car door for her. "Right now I'm worried about you."

Ashleigh looked up at the pasture. Her father already had Moe loaded in the trailer, and now he was inching his way down the hill, carefully avoiding as much rough ground as he could.

Poor Moe. Ashleigh imagined the hurt little pony all alone in the back of the trailer, not knowing what was going on. Fresh tears welled up in her eyes.

"I'm so sorry, Moe," she whispered, and climbed into the car. "Mom, I'm sorry," she repeated

"I know you wouldn't hurt Moe on purpose," Mrs. Griffen said. "We'll talk about this later. Right now I want to get you taken care of."

Ashleigh stared out the window as they headed to the medical center in town. She didn't want to talk about it later. "I was stupid, okay? I know it. It's just hard riding a pony I'm too big for when Mona's cantering around on Frisky. I was mad. That's why I galloped Moe down the hill."

Mrs. Griffen was silent for several minutes. Ashleigh was sure her mom was figuring out a suitable punishment. Then Mrs. Griffen sighed.

"I know it was difficult for you to give up Lightning. Especially since we can't afford to buy you a good horse right now to replace her." She reached over to rest a hand on Ashleigh's knee. "I do understand, Ash."

"So I'm not in trouble?" Ashleigh held on to a faint glimmer of hope.

Mrs. Griffen shook her head and pulled into the medical center parking lot. "Let's get you checked out and see what the vet says about Moe before we talk about anything, okay?"

"I don't deserve a horse, anyway," Ashleigh muttered, climbing from the car. "It's a good thing I gave Lightning to Hopewell. I'd probably do something horrible to her, too."

Mrs. Griffen wrapped her arm around Ashleigh's shoulders and they headed into the emergency-room entrance. "Beating yourself up isn't going to make anything better, Ash. You acted without thinking and risked Moe's safety. Maybe now you'll remember you need to put the animal's well-being first. Now sit down while I get you signed in."

Once she had been X-rayed and her scratches cleaned a second time, the doctor flashed a little light in her eyes, checked her lungs, and asked her to wriggle her arms and legs. She wanted to tell him to leave her alone, but she didn't dare mouth off.

"Kids heal fast," she heard him tell Mrs. Griffen.

"No concussion, no broken bones. Just keep the scratches clean and she'll be fine in no time."

Ashleigh was relieved to get back in the car and head home. When they pulled into their drive, she could see the two-horse trailer parked under the trees.

Ashleigh was out of the car before her mother shut off the engine. She dashed toward the barn.

"Dad!" she yelled, rushing inside.

"I'm in the isolation stall," he answered.

"How's Moe?" Ashleigh called. When he didn't respond, Ashleigh raced down the aisle in a panic, her mother right behind her. Her heart was pounding when she skidded to a stop in front of the large stall and looked inside.

Moe stood with his foreleg in a bucket of ice water. Her father was crouched in the bedding beside the pony, stroking his shoulder. Ashleigh felt her shoulders sag with relief. Ice wasn't the treatment for a fractured leg. "His leg isn't broken."

"Be thankful," her father said, rising and stepping out of the stall. He looked closely at Ashleigh, frowning at what he saw. "What did the doctor say about you?"

"That I'll heal fast," she said. "Just a few scratches." She stepped into Moe's stall and knelt down next to him. "Poor Moe," she said softly. "Do you forgive me?" Moe looked at her with his soft brown eyes and nuzzled her. Ashleigh sighed with relief.

"I'm glad you're all right," her father said. "Moe, on the other hand, has a severely pulled tendon that's going to take a while to heal. He has a few stitches in one knee, and they're both badly scraped. He's going to be out of action for a while."

"Dad, I didn't mean to hurt him," Ashleigh said, looking up at her father.

"I know." Mr. Griffen stepped into the stall with her and rubbed Moe's shoulder. "But you were reckless, and he's the one who's suffering."

Ashleigh dropped her head. She couldn't cry any more. Her eyes were out of tears. "I know it's all my fault," she said.

"It was an accident, Ashleigh. But what were you thinking, to run him down a hill like that? You know better."

Ashleigh cringed at her father's voice. "I guess I wasn't thinking. I just did it. We've run down hills before and Moe never fell. I didn't know there were woodchuck holes there."

Her father exhaled hard, and her mother reached over the stall door and caught his arm. "I need to return the Gardeners' car, Derek," she said in a quiet voice. "You can follow me over so I don't have to walk back. It's getting late." She glanced at Ashleigh. "We'll talk to you when we get back."

"Moe needs another fifteen minutes in the ice," Mr. Griffen said to Ashleigh. "Kurt will be done with the hay inventory by then and he can help you rewrap it." He stepped out of the stall. "Caroline started dinner," he told his wife. "She's had Rory up at the house all afternoon. He's very upset."

Her parents headed out of the barn, their voices trailing off. Ashleigh stepped to Moe's side. She looked into his trusting brown eyes and felt guilty all over again.

"Moe, I'm so sorry," she said, hugging Moe's neck. The pony seemed to forgive her, nickering and gratefully accepting the carrot Ashleigh offered. Ashleigh rubbed her hand over his neck and scratched Moe's ears. She looked down at his injured leg, immersed in icy water. Exhausted, Ashleigh sank down into the bedding in Moe's stall. The pony munched his hay while Ashleigh looked on, making sure his injured leg stayed inside the bucket of ice.

Pounding footsteps made Ashleigh sit up quickly. She could hear Rory yelling before he reached the barn. "You hurt my pony!"

Ashleigh hunched her shoulders and bit at her lower lip. *Here goes,* she thought. The stall door burst open and Rory stood in the doorway, glaring down at his sister. His little face was tearstained, and his lower lip quivered.

"Liar," he said accusingly. "You promised not to hurt Moe, but you hurt him bad. You're mean, Ashleigh."

Ashleigh stared up at her brother. "Rory, it was an accident. I didn't mean to hurt Moe."

"You did." Fresh tears ran down Rory's face, and Ashleigh felt a new supply of her own start flowing.

Caroline dashed up behind them. "Ashleigh couldn't help it, Rory. It was an accident. Dad already told you that."

"I don't care," Rory screamed. Ashleigh stood up as Caroline pulled him from the stall.

Kurt came down the aisle, moving quickly. He glanced at Ashleigh's scratched, tear-streaked face and frowned. "Are you okay, Ashleigh?"

"I'm fine," she snapped. *Why does everyone have to keep asking that?*

Kurt looked down at Rory and shook his head. "Why don't you all go on up to the house?" he said, stepping into Moe's stall and pulling the door shut behind him. "I'll finish taking care of Moe's ice soak, and then I'll rewrap his leg."

Ashleigh started from the barn without a word.

Caroline hooked an arm around Rory's waist and hefted him off the ground. In spite of his squirming and thrashing, she managed to get him outside before he struggled from her grip. He charged at Ashleigh, who took a step back, even though Rory was only half her size.

"I told you not to take him," he yelled. "You're too big for him now. I told you and you wouldn't listen. You're bad and mean. You should have listened to me."

He began punching at Ashleigh, who couldn't bring herself to stop him, even though Rory's hard little fists hurt.

Caroline grabbed Rory. "Stop it!" She glanced at Ashleigh and grimaced. "He was in a frenzy all afternoon, worried about Moe."

Ashleigh shrugged. She felt too terrible to speak. Rory was right. She was bad.

Caroline headed for the house, Rory firmly in her grip.

Rory glared at her from over Caroline's shoulder. "You said you wouldn't hurt him. I hate you, Ashleigh. I really hate you."

Ashleigh went straight up to her room and got her diary out of her desk drawer. She didn't write in it every day, only when something especially good or bad happened. She curled up on the bed with her new kitten, who snuggled next to her and started to purr. "At least you're not mad at me," Ashleigh said as she stroked the kitten's fur. A moment later she opened her diary and began to write.

Dear Diary,

It's been a very bad day. I got into a lot of trouble. I was racing Mona. I shouldn't have been, but I was angry that she had this gorgeous new Thoroughbred named Frisky and I was still riding a pony. I missed Lightning and I wished I hadn't given her to Hopewell. Then I pushed Moe too hard, and he stepped in a hole and fell. His knees are all cut up, and he pulled a tendon in his right foreleg. I fell off and now I have scratches on my face, but that doesn't matter as much as Moe. Rory's so mad at me for hurting Moe and my parents sounded angry, too. I guess I'm in for a big lecture. I feel so bad. Why did I do such a stupid thing?

I just feel like crying.

Ashleigh closed the diary and went to the bathroom to shower. When she got a good look at her face in the mirror, she cringed. "I just wish this whole day would go away!" she cried to her reflection.

4

Ashleigh barely recognized herself. The doctor had bandaged the cheek that had the worst of the scratches, but her eyes were bruised and swollen, and she had a fat lip, too.

"At least I don't have to go to school like this," she muttered, turning away from her horrifying image. After her shower, Ashleigh dressed slowly and sat on the edge of her bed, feeling as though everything had become a bad dream. When she heard her parents getting dinner ready downstairs, she debated hiding under her bed. Instead she left her room and headed down to face them. They sat at the kitchen table, talking in low voices. When Ashleigh walked into the room, they both glanced up at her. Neither of them looked very happy.

Her father pointed at an empty chair. "Sit down, Ashleigh," he said in a serious voice.

Ashleigh couldn't tell whether he was angry or concerned. Reluctantly, she sat and folded her hands on her lap. *Here it comes.* She tried to imagine the worst possible punishment, but none of it seemed bad enough. She had hurt Moe, and she had to live with that.

"Caroline told us about Rory," her mother said. "He's asleep now. He was worn out, Ashleigh. He spent the whole afternoon not knowing what was going on with Moe, and he was worried and upset. You know he didn't mean it when he said he hated you."

"He should hate me, I deserve it," Ashleigh muttered, dropping her chin. She stared at the floor, wishing it would open up and swallow her.

"That's enough of that." At her father's sharp tone, Ashleigh jumped and looked up at him.

"No one should hate anyone, and it sounds to me like you're feeling sorry for yourself," Mr. Griffen said. "We know you had a rough time making the decision about Lightning, but you let feeling sorry for yourself get in the way of Moe's well-being. Now it's time to start acting responsibly.

"First, you are in charge of Moe's care—all the work like changing his knee bandages and keeping track of the time his leg is in the ice bucket. Since it's still vacation week, you'll be responsible for him full time."

"Okay," Ashleigh said. "I'll take good care of him, I promise."

Ashleigh picked up Prince. "Let's go check on Moe before bedtime," she said, carrying the kitten downstairs. She slipped into a jacket and went down to the barn. Inside, the aisle was quiet. Ashleigh walked slowly, inhaling the horse smells.

Being around the Thoroughbreds made her feel better, but nothing had changed. She had no horse to ride, and she was sure she would be banned forever from getting on Moe again. She stopped in front of his stall. The pony nickered softly to her, and Ashleigh slipped him the carrot she had tucked in her pocket.

"He seems to be doing pretty well," Kurt said, strolling down from where he had been checking on the broodmares for the night.

"I'm glad," Ashleigh said quietly, not looking up at the stable hand.

"I know you must feel rotten about this," Kurt said.

"Don't you want to tell me how dumb I was, too?"

"No." Kurt squeezed Ashleigh's shoulder. "Listen, I'm going to Hopewell tomorrow. Do you feel like coming with me? We can go between Moe's times in the ice bucket."

Kurt was probably just trying to be nice and make her feel better, but Ashleigh was grateful. Maybe seeing Kira would cheer her up. She smiled at Kurt.

"Sure, that would be fun," she said, picking Prince

Charming up. "I'd better go up to the house now. Good night, Kurt."

Ashleigh walked through the rest of the barn, giving each of the broodmares a gentle pat on the nose, pausing to visit the foals and press her face to a few soft muzzles. "Good night, Wanderer," she said, stroking the mare's black cheek. In the next stall Jolita whickered softly, and Ashleigh paused to give her chestnut coat a pat. Then she headed out of the barn and back to the house.

"Mona didn't call, did she?" Ashleigh asked Caroline, who was curled up on her own bed, reading a teen magazine.

Caroline shrugged. "I don't know," she said, glancing over at Ashleigh. "Boy, you really messed up your face, didn't you, Ash? I hope it doesn't scar."

"And what if it does?" Ashleigh snapped. "I don't care. I'm going to be a jockey, not a model." She grabbed her pajamas from the laundry piled on the floor and headed into the bathroom.

When she woke up the next morning, Ashleigh thought for a few seconds that she had just dreamed the awful things that had happened. But there were specks of blood on her pillowcase from the scratches on her face. She sank back against the bed and sighed. Prince Charming, who had been curled up beside her all night, began purring, and she stroked his soft coat. She hated to get up and face everyone again, but she needed to go to the barn and take care of Moe. She saw by the clock that her parents had let her sleep late, even though she usually woke up early on her own.

Caroline was still asleep, so Ashleigh dressed quickly and hurried out of the room. At least she was still on Christmas vacation, so she didn't have to see the kids at school with her bashed-up face. She hoped it would be healed by next week.

Kurt and her parents were already at work when she came into the barn. Kurt walked past her, leading Slewette, a dark bay, and My Georgina, a shiny chestnut. The mares wore their warm winter turnout blankets. Althea saw Ashleigh and gave a hopeful nicker.

"Sorry, sweetie," Ashleigh said, giving her a quick pat. "I don't have any treats for you right now."

Several of the mares were already outside. Ashleigh's mother walked by, leading Wanderer. She stopped when Ashleigh got close. "Your face looks better already," Mrs. Griffen said. "How are you feeling?"

"Fine." Ashleigh hurried down the aisle to the isolation stall, where Moe was pulling hay out of the hay net Kurt had hung in his stall. The pony grunted a welcome to Ashleigh when she came into the stall. She dug a small apple from her pocket and handed it to him.

Moe was used to getting lots of treats. He quickly ate the apple, then went back to his hay. His leg wasn't due to be iced for another hour, so Ashleigh went to the tack room to gather what she needed to clean his scraped knees. She returned to his stall with the antiseptic ointment, a bucket of warm water, a clean sponge, and towels.

Moe continued to work on his hay while Ashleigh knelt in the straw bedding. She thoroughly cleaned both knees, dried them, and applied a thick layer of ointment. She had just put the supplies away and was getting a wheelbarrow and pitchfork to clean his stall when her father walked up.

"How's he doing?" Mr. Griffen asked.

"He looks okay," Ashleigh said. "But I need help with the bandage for his stitches."

"I'll take care of it," Mr. Griffen told her. "You go finish your other chores."

Ashleigh began cleaning the broodmares' stalls. She and Caroline each had four to clean, and Rory had two. Her parents cleaned the weanlings' stalls. As Ashleigh pushed the wheelbarrow to her first stall, she passed Rory, who only scowled at her and stomped past, heading for Moe's stall.

After she finished her stalls, Ashleigh noticed Rory hadn't started on his yet. She quickly finished his work, hoping it would help him forgive her. If anything, it eased Ashleigh's guilt to do Rory's chores for him. She hurried to the house for a bucket of ice. Maybe she could ask Rory to help her ice Moe's leg, Ashleigh thought. Rory would like that.

But when she returned to the stall, Rory was gone. She tried not to be upset. He didn't even care that she'd cleaned his stupid stalls. Of course, she told herself, that didn't make up for her hurting Moe. But it had to help a little.

She brushed Moe while she waited for the time to pass, working a comb through his thick mane and massaging his little back with a soft rubber currycomb. Moe didn't seem to mind the extra attention.

When the treatment time was up, Ashleigh lifted Moe's leg from the ice bucket and changed the bulky leg wrap. She gave the pony a kiss on his nose, whispering, "I really am so sorry, Moe." Then she slipped out of the stall and carried the bucket back to the house.

Ashleigh's mother was in the kitchen, pouring coffee into a thermos.

"Rory is never going to forgive me, Mom. He's really mad."

Mrs. Griffen pulled Ashleigh close, giving her a reassuring hug. "Give him time, sweetheart. Rory loves you. He'll forgive you. Just give him a little time." She stepped back and lifted Ashleigh's chin with her finger. "Your face still looks pretty messy, Ash. Kurt said he invited you to go to Hopewell for a couple of hours. Are you sure you're up to it?"

Ashleigh thought of the kids at Hopewell. Some were in wheelchairs, and some wore scarves because the treatments they received made their hair fall out. Her little scratches wouldn't matter to them. "I'm fine, Mom. Is it okay if I go? If there's more work to do here, I'll stay."

"No. Your father and I are going to finish evaluating stud fees and decide which stallions we want to use this year."

"What about Wanderer?" Ashleigh asked, thinking about their best broodmare.

"We'll pay high stud fees to breed her to the best, since her yearling brought such a high price at auction last fall," her mother said. "We hope this year's foal turns out as well as her last colt."

"Tonka sure has turned out great," Ashleigh said. "Everyone says so. I think all of Wanderer's babies are going to be champions."

"That would be a good thing for Edgardale," Mrs.

Griffen said with a smile. She picked up the thermos of coffee and headed back for the barn.

Ashleigh followed her mother down to the barn, where Kurt was waiting in his old pickup.

When they arrived at Hopewell, Kurt parked in front of the large stone house that was the facility's main building. Since it had been a private estate before the cancer center took it over, Hopewell looked more like a mansion than a medical facility.

Ashleigh climbed from the truck and looked toward the barn.

"I'm going inside," Kurt said. "Do you want to see Lightning first?"

"Of course," Ashleigh said, starting along the tree-lined drive that led to Hopewell's large barn.

"I'll let Kira know you're out there," Kurt said, and started up the walk.

Ashleigh stopped and glanced over her shoulder. She wavered for a moment, torn between wanting to see the mare and going inside to wish the staff and children a merry Christmas. Even though in her heart she wanted to see Lightning first, she turned and followed Kurt into the house.

From the entryway, Ashleigh could see into the large community living room. A tall Christmas tree took up one corner, and several kids were in the room, playing games or watching television.

"Ashleigh, up here!"

Ashleigh looked up the wide, graceful stairway that curved to the second floor. Kira stood at the top of the stairs, waving her arm. "Come on up and see my room!"

Ashleigh hurried up the stairs.

"Wow," Kira said, looking at Ashleigh's face. "Nice scratches. What happened to you?"

"Thanks," Ashleigh said with a wry grin. "It's a long story."

Kira wore a bright scarf to cover her almost bald head. She had lost her hair during chemotherapy, and it was just beginning to grow back. Ashleigh didn't mind Kira looking at her face. Kira knew how it felt to look different.

They headed along the hall to the room that was Kira's as long as she needed to stay at Hopewell. As they walked, Ashleigh told her everything that had happened.

When they stepped inside Kira's room, Ashleigh looked around. "This is really neat," she said, admiring the bright colors and the horse posters that covered most of the walls. A row of horse statues lined the wide windowsill. Still, Ashleigh reminded herself, this was really just a hospital room.

"Do you like it?" Kira asked.

"Love it," Ashleigh said. "But don't you miss your room at home?"

Kira's eyes widened and she nodded. "A lot. Actually, it's only about half this big and the carpet isn't very nice, but it's home. I try not to think about it, though. The doctors say a good attitude is important, so I try to be positive."

Ashleigh thought about her own attitude the last few days and winced. If a good attitude could help with something as serious as cancer, it had to help with a lot of other things.

"So," Kira said, her voice bright again, "does your face hurt? It looks kind of sore."

Ashleigh touched her cheek lightly and shook her head. "It's fine. It just looks bad. Moe's the one who really got hurt. He had to have stitches."

"Poor little pony," Kira said. "Give him a carrot for me when you get home, okay?" She peered out her window, which overlooked the barn. "Now, come on. Let's go see Lighting." Kira led the way out of her bedroom.

Ashleigh was glad Kira had suggested it first. She didn't want to be rude, but she did want to see Lightning. It would be the first time she'd seen her since the mare had left Edgardale. Ashleigh hoped she could handle it. She wasn't feeling very positive at the moment.

They hurried out of the house and went straight to the mare's stall in the spacious, well-lit barn. When Lightning saw Ashleigh, she gave a delighted nicker and rushed to the stall door.

Ashleigh rubbed her hand down the mare's nose. Lightning bobbed her head, pressing her nose into Ashleigh's hair and snuffling. "Hi, pretty girl," Ashleigh murmured to her. "I'm so glad to see you."

"She misses you," Kira said, petting the mare's neck.

"I miss her, too," Ashleigh admitted. She was happy to see how well Lightning looked. The mare's white coat shone with good health, and her eyes were bright and alert. Ashleigh wrapped her arms around the horse's neck and hugged her, fighting back tears when Lightning pressed her head against Ashleigh's shoulder, as if she were trying to hug back.

"Oh, poor Ashleigh," she heard Kira murmur sympathetically.

Ashleigh let go of Lightning's neck, and the mare nudged her chest inquisitively. Swallowing the lump in her throat, Ashleigh rubbed Lightning's nose and smiled at Kira.

"I really miss her," she said. "But I think Lightning belongs here. You guys are taking such great care of her."

"I'm glad you feel that way," Kira said. "I know having Lightning here is helping me a lot. I spend all my free time in the barn or outside with her. But if you wanted her back, it would be selfish of us to keep her. Everyone would understand if you wanted to take her back. She seems so excited to see you."

Then Ashleigh noticed for the first time the healthy color in Kira's face and the sparkle in her eyes. Lightning really was helping Kira get better.

"No, I'm glad Lightning's here," Ashleigh said firmly, meaning it with all her heart.

Then she heard Kurt calling her name. "Oh . . . I have to get going," Ashleigh said reluctantly. "It's time to ice Moe's leg." She fondled Lightning's ears and ran her hand through the mare's silky white mane. After giving the horse one last pat, Ashleigh put her arms around Kira, hugging her friend close. "I'm glad Lightning is so good for you."

Ashleigh looked away quickly as she felt tears fill her eyes. Lightning wasn't hers anymore, and she would never have her back. She hurried out the door, wondering how much worse she was going to feel before things got better. The hard part was, there was only one thing that could make her feel better: a horse.

5

"Ash, can you grab that wheelbarrow and finish cleaning Zip Away's stall? I just sent Caroline up to the
house to put on a fresh pot of coffee." Mrs. Griffen
laughed as she threw another pitchfork of bedding
into her own wheelbarrow. "I don't drink it all, but on
these cold winter days, it feels good to wrap my hands
around a nice hot mug."

"Sure, Mom." Ashleigh said, knowing her mother
drank every drop. She pushed her sister's abandoned
wheelbarrow down the aisle. Even on crisp winter
mornings, the barn was still the best place in the
world to be. She knew Caroline would linger as long
as possible in the house. Her sister would rather clean
the kitchen than muck out a stall any day.

"By the way, Ash, you've been a great help the last
couple of days," Mrs. Griffen said.

Ashleigh stopped the wheelbarrow in front of the

unfinished stall, beaming at the compliment. "I'm trying."

"It shows. Your father and I can see how hard you're working."

Ashleigh concentrated on stripping the rest of the soiled bedding, then headed down the aisle with the loaded wheelbarrow.

"Oh, Ash," Mrs. Griffen said when Ashleigh walked past her, "I do have one extra project for you."

Ashleigh sighed. She was trying to keep a positive attitude, but it seemed as though her parents were really piling on the little jobs for her to do. She'd already polished the buckles on the halters they used for the yearlings at auction time, and then she'd helped her mother tidy the tack room. It could have been worse, Ashleigh thought. They could have asked her to clean under her bed or, worse, her closet. "Okay," Ashleigh said, smiling at her mother, "but school's starting again, so I'll have less time for—"

"We need to get one of the empty stalls fixed up" her mother interrupted. "We're bringing in a new horse in a couple of days."

Ashleigh's jaw dropped. "A new broodmare? Why didn't anyone tell me about it?"

Her mother shrugged. "We weren't sure until today. So now you need to get the stall in tip-top shape for the new horse. Don't just stand around. You have a lot of work to do."

Her mother had a twinkle in her eye that meant something else was going on. Ashleigh hurried outside to dump the load of bedding, then rushed back inside, cornering her mother in the barn office. "Who is the new mare? What are her bloodlines? Is she bred yet? Are we buying her?"

Mrs. Griffen laughed, raising her hands in front of her. "Whoa! Slow down. The answers are: you'll find out, I don't know, no, and no. Now are you satisfied?"

"No!" Ashleigh propped her hands on her hips and pursed her lips. "That just makes more questions."

"First things first. Pick a good stall and get it ready. I'll answer your questions when you're done."

Ashleigh hesitated, eager to pump her mother for more information. She started to open her mouth, but her mother angled her head and narrowed her eyes. The look always made Ashleigh think of the boss mare warning off the other horses. If her mother could have pinned her ears back in warning, she just might have. Ashleigh left the office and looked through the empty stalls, trying to choose the best one for the mystery horse.

When she saw her little brother coming out of Moe's stall, she started to follow him. He hadn't given her a chance to apologize. Now was as good a time as any.

"Rory," she called. He glanced at her, then looked away and started down the aisle. Ashleigh rushed after him. "Please talk to me," she begged. "You can't stay mad at me forever."

"Yes, I can," he said, turning to face her. "You hurt Moe," he shouted, and took off at a run. Ashleigh started to chase after him but changed her mind. As soon as she finished the stall for the new horse, she'd find Rory and get things settled with him.

Two hours later, the stall was ready to go. The floor was covered with fresh bedding, banked up on the sides and heaped high in the corners to prevent the horse from getting cast—wedged in the corners of the stall— if she lay down or rolled. A clean feed pan and water bucket were in place, and an empty hay net hung near the door. All the stall needed now was a horse.

Caroline strolled by the stall, her hair up in curlers and her new sweater peeking out from beneath her coat. "Nice job, Ash," she said. "Maybe if you used a pitchfork to clean your half of the room, it would look that good."

Ashleigh wrinkled her nose at her sister, but before she could say anything, Mrs. Griffen stepped out of the office.

"What's Rory up to?" she asked Caroline.

Caroline's eyes widened. "He's down here," she said.

"No, he's not," Ashleigh broke in. "I saw him leave the barn hours ago."

"He didn't come back to the house?" Mrs. Griffen directed a worried frown at Caroline.

"He did," she said defensively. "But that was a long time ago. He came in, got Prince Charming, and left again. I watched him from the window. He was headed this way."

"He took my kitten?" Ashleigh demanded. "If he hurts Prince—"

Her mother stopped her with a wave of her hand. "Ashleigh, Rory is not going to do anything to your cat. He probably just took him out to play."

"But Rory's still mad at me, and it's too cold for Prince Charming to be outside. . . ." Ashleigh's voice trailed off.

"Caroline, you look everywhere in the house," Mrs. Griffen said. "Ashleigh, you search this barn from top to bottom. I'm going to look outside and down toward the road."

Caroline dashed out one end of the barn, and Mrs. Griffen hurried out the other. Ashleigh stood motionless, thinking.

Suddenly she dropped her pitchfork, which clattered to the concrete floor, and ran for the steps to the hayloft.

"Rory," she called, stepping into the dark loft. The sweet hay smell filled the air, and the soft meow of a barn cat caught her attention.

"Here, kitty, kitty," she called. Two of the barn cats leaped onto bales of hay and slunk back and forth, demanding to be petted. Ashleigh ran her hand along one sleek back and called again. Another meow answered her—a kitten's meow, small and soft. She walked around the wall of hay and in the direction of the sound.

"Shhh." Rory's voice was louder than the kitten's cry.

A smile played on Ashleigh's mouth. The back corner of the loft, where the eaves met the floor, had always been her favorite place to hide. The bales of hay formed a tunnel between the roof and floor. Ashleigh dropped to her knees and crawled behind the hay.

Rory was huddled against a hay bale, Prince Charming in his lap. Ashleigh sighed with relief.

"You scared everyone, Rory. Mom and Caro are running around like crazy trying to find you."

In the gloom, Rory's lower lip quivered. "I was mad, Ash. I was going to hide Prince Charming with the barn cats, but they didn't like him, so I took him back here to keep him safe. Then I kind of fell asleep."

Ashleigh extended a hand to him, and slowly he reached out. Their fingertips touched; then Ashleigh caught his wrist and tugged her brother forward. Ashleigh backed out of the hole, and Rory crawled after her, the kitten still tucked inside his jacket.

Rory stood up and looked up at her, a fat tear rolling down his cheek. Prince Charming didn't seem to have suffered from his adventure. He nestled under Rory's chin and began to purr.

Ashleigh stood straight and looked down at her little brother. "I don't blame you for being so mad at me," she said firmly. "I hurt Moe. And I'm doing everything I can to get him better. Moe forgave me, Rory. I think you should, too."

Rory's lip quivered.

"Please, Rory. I love you. You're the best brother I have."

Rory frowned. "I'm your only brother," he said.

"And I don't want you mad at me. Moe's knee is almost better. Pretty soon you'll be able to go out on him again."

"You won't ride him anymore, will you?"

Ashleigh sighed. This was harder than she had expected. But Rory was right. She had no business riding the little pony. Moe was his now. She raised her right hand and looked her brother square in the eyes. "I promise I will never ride Moe again, Rory."

"Okay. I forgive you."

Ashleigh exhaled hard. Having Rory glare at her every time she walked past him the last couple of days had been horrible. At least that was taken care of now. But she still needed to talk to Mona. It seemed as though apologizing should get easier with practice, but she was getting tired of it.

She bent down and gave her brother a hug. "Do you want to help me ice Moe's leg in a little while? He really likes the attention. I brush him while his leg is soaking. Have you seen how nice his coat looks?"

Rory smiled. "I want to help."

"Good. Right now we need to let Mom and Caro know you're okay. I'll take care of Prince Charming," she said, prying the kitten from her brother's coat. She left Rory at Moe's stall and ran off to find her mother, the kitten hugged to her chest. Mrs. Griffen was walking back from the paddocks, worry lines creasing her face.

Ashleigh waved and yelled, "Found him, Mom!"

Mrs. Griffen ran back to the barn. "Thank goodness," she said. "You tell Caroline. I'm going to have a little talk with Rory about disappearing like that."

"At least he's talking to me again," Ashleigh said

happily. She went to find her sister and put her kitten in the house.

When Ashleigh returned to the barn, Rory was in Moe's stall, brushing the pony, and Mrs. Griffen was in the barn office, a mug of coffee in her hands. She smiled up at Ashleigh, who stopped in the doorway. "I'm glad you were able to work things out with Rory. Things seem to be looking up for you, don't they?"

"What do you mean?"

Mrs. Griffen took a slow sip of coffee and eyed Ashleigh from over the cup's rim. "Ash, the stall you just fixed up is for a riding horse, not a broodmare."

Ashleigh gaped at her mother, speechless. Her brain couldn't form any words, and even if it could have, her jaw seemed to be stuck.

Mrs. Griffen laughed and set the cup down. "We heard about this mare a couple of weeks ago. She's part Thoroughbred, and the owners have been very careful about finding a new home for her. They told us she belonged to their daughter, who's away at college, and she hasn't been ridden for about a year. They wanted her to go to someone who would take the time to get her back into shape and work with her. When they heard about you and Lightning, they wanted to know if you would be interested." Mrs. Griffen's face turned serious for a moment. "When you had the accident with Moe, we weren't sure if you were ready to take on another horse. But you've really turned around, and we know it's what you wanted all along."

Ashleigh felt her heart soar. A horse! "Oh, Mom, thank you! Thank you so much!" Ashleigh rushed around the desk and threw her arms around her mother's neck. Mrs. Griffen hugged her back.

"The deal, Ashleigh, is that you will maintain your grades and keep up this good attitude, and that you will work with Moe and Rory. No neglecting any of your regular responsibilities just because you have a horse to use."

"To use? Won't she be mine?" Ashleigh knew she sounded spoiled, but her mother had made it sound as though the horse would belong to her.

"Not until you prove to us how responsible you are."

"No problem!" Ashleigh ran from the office and down the hall. She had to call Mona and tell her the good news. She started for the house, then remembered Rory and Moe. She raced the rest of the way to the house for a bucket of ice, then jogged back to the barn, where Rory was still in the stall with Moe.

With Rory helping, it took longer than usual to ice Moe's leg. They treated his knees and rebandaged his leg, then Rory headed for the house to play with his Christmas toys, leaving Ashleigh to pick up the supplies.

When Ashleigh finally took the ice bucket back to the house, she hurried to the phone to call Mona. Mona was out with Frisky, but Mrs. Gardener promised to have her call when she got in.

Eager to share her great news with someone, Ashleigh called Hopewell and asked for Kira.

In a minute someone else came on the line. "Ashleigh? This is Sally, the physical therapist. How are you doing?"

"I'm fine," Ashleigh said, confused. "Where's Kira? I've got great news for her. Is everything all right?"

There was a moment's pause, then Sally spoke again. "She's at the hospital, Ashleigh."

Ashleigh's excitement left her in an instant. She closed her eyes. "No, she can't be! I just saw her a couple of days ago. She looked great." *Please let Kira be all right,* Ashleigh wished silently.

To her surprise, Sally gave a little laugh. "It's not necessarily bad to be at the hospital. She went to have a series of tests done. They want to see how she's coming along with her treatment. She'll be back in a couple of days, don't worry."

Ashleigh hung up, her excited mood dampened by

her worry about Kira. She didn't care what Sally said. Going to the hospital could not be a good thing. Maybe Kurt would be able to tell her more. She pulled her jacket on again and headed for the barn.

Her parents were in their office, going over some of the endless paperwork the farm generated. She walked past the doorway and up the stairs leading to Kurt's apartment. She tapped at his door, feeling strange. She'd never visited the apartment before.

In moments Kurt opened the door and frowned down at her. "What's wrong, Ashleigh?"

Ashleigh hesitated. Maybe Kurt wouldn't want to talk about chemotherapy and hospitals. His own daughter had died of leukemia almost two years ago. Ashleigh regretted bothering him. "Never mind," she said. "Sorry I bugged you." She started to turn away.

"Wait." His voice stopped her, and Ashleigh looked back.

"I have a little time if you want to talk. Why don't we go for a walk down by the paddocks? The mares are going to need to come in soon, anyway. It looks like it's ready to start raining any minute."

Ashleigh and Kurt made their way along the grassy lane between the paddocks. Kurt didn't say anything, just strolled along with his hands in his pockets, looking at the fences and the horses.

Finally Ashleigh couldn't hold back any longer. Her words came out in a rush. "I'm scared for Kira. I called to tell her about the new horse coming, and Sally said she's in the hospital. Sally said it was okay, just for tests, but I don't think they'd tell me the truth. If Kira's in the hospital, it must mean she's getting worse instead of better."

She looked up at Kurt, who had a sad, distant look on his face. When he looked down at her, he forced a smile, but Ashleigh could still see the sorrow in his eyes. "I don't think Sally would lie to you, Ashleigh. But if it makes you feel better, I'll call and see what I can find out."

Ashleigh felt a rush of gratitude. "Thank you," she breathed. They walked back to the barn. Ashleigh glanced up at the gathering clouds. They loomed dark and heavy over the farm, and she shivered, pulling her jacket close.

Ashleigh found a copy of the *Daily Racing Form* in her parents' office and sat down to look through it while she waited for Kurt to call Hopewell from his apartment. Her thoughts raced, and she couldn't keep her mind on her reading. *A new horse was coming to Edgardale. . . . Kira might be really sick. . . . What name should she give the new horse? . . .*

The wind picked up with a sudden gust, and the

office window rattled. Ashleigh jumped from her chair and ran outside, joining her parents and Kurt, who hurried to move the mares and weanlings inside. They were so busy getting the twenty horses in before the rain started that she didn't even have time to look at Kurt.

Just as Mr. Griffen was bringing the last of the horses into the barn, the rain began to fall. Slewette pranced sideways as a few raindrops plopped onto her blanket, but Mr. Griffen held her head firmly, keeping her from trying to take off down the barn aisle.

"They'll be stuck inside for a while," Mrs. Griffen observed, looking at the sheets of cold rain driving down outside the barn. Kurt pulled the big sliding door shut. "Good day for fish," he said with a grin, wiping a few raindrops from his forehead.

Ashleigh held Slewette's stall door open while her father led the mare inside. Kurt still seemed to be in a very good mood after calling Hopewell. She hadn't had a chance to talk to him, but Ashleigh hoped his joking mood meant he had good news. Maybe Kira really was fine.

She hurried to help fill hay nets and feed pans, checking each horse's feeding schedule as she scooped grain, vitamins, and supplements into the pans.

Soon the chores were completed and the Griffens

prepared to head for the house. Ashleigh held back, to check on Moe one last time before leaving.

While she was in his stall Kurt strolled up, a grin on his face. "I talked to Sally," he said. "They sent Kira in for tests because she's doing so well. They think she'll be able to go home soon. Lightning really made a big difference in her treatment—she's made huge strides—but the best place for her is home."

Ashleigh felt elated. "I'm so glad," she said, stepping out of Moe's stall and latching the door. "Thanks for checking, Kurt."

"No problem," he said, "and don't worry about Lightning. The other kids at Hopewell will pay her tons of attention." Kurt headed for his apartment. Ashleigh watched him go. His step seemed lighter, his shoulders less stooped. Maybe Kurt had been worried about Kira, too.

Ashleigh dashed through the rain to the house and arrived soaking and breathless. "I should have just walked," she said, pulling off her soggy jacket. "I couldn't have gotten any wetter."

"Get out of those wet clothes and dry your hair," her mother said. "Dinner will be ready in a few minutes."

Ashleigh checked the answering machine. Mona had left a message, so she quickly dialed the Gardeners' house. Ashleigh's life seemed to have turned around in a day. She couldn't wait to speak to her friend.

"Mona?"

"Yeah?"

"I'm sorry I got so mad at you when Moe got hurt. I was upset."

"I know," Mona said. "My mom said it was hard for you to see me riding Frisky when you had to give up Lightning. I'm sorry, too, Ash. I hate when we fight. I miss talking to you."

"Me too. Can you come over tomorrow?"

"Sure. With this weather I won't be riding for a few days."

"Well, guess what?" Ashleigh said. "You won't be riding alone."

"What are you talking about?"

Ashleigh told Mona what she knew about the new horse. "We'll both have real horses to ride. And this one will be ours to keep."

"Do you know her name?"

"I've decided to call her Stardust," Ashleigh said. "My mom says she's a solid chestnut with a white star on her forehead and a white stripe and snip on her nose. She and Frisky will look great together."

"How tall is she?"

"I don't know," Ashleigh said. "I didn't think to ask.

I know she's part Thoroughbred, so she can't be too small."

"As soon as she gets here we'll go for a great ride," Mona said. "I can hardly wait. Oh, Ash, I'm so happy for you!"

Ashleigh hung up the phone smiling. Kira had been right. A good attitude did seem to make a big difference. Her life was getting better all the time.

6

Ashleigh glared at the icy rain streaking the living room window. It had been raining for two days. Not being able to go outside was turning her Christmas vacation into a real drag.

But as soon as the weather improved, her parents would go and get Stardust in the trailer. She looked down at the drawing pad on her lap, where she had tried to draw what she thought the mare would look like. Her horse drawings weren't very good. *It's a good thing I want to be a jockey and not an artist,* she thought, closing the pad.

She had already soaked Moe's leg twice that day and mucked out her stalls. Now, with so much time and nothing to do, she flipped through the pages of a horse magazine, looking closely at every chestnut she found.

An article on steeplechasing caught her attention,

and she read it through. The photos showed beautiful, powerful horses sailing over huge brush fences. "That looks scary, but I might try a little jumping," she said to Prince Charming, who was curled up on her lap. "Stardust has lots of experience, so she should be able to do just about anything. She's going to be a great horse, and she's going to love me. I just know it." Ashleigh let her head drop back and gazed at the ceiling. In her imagination, she and Stardust had just flown past the half-mile marker. She could hear the track announcer describing their perfect moves as they edged towards the front of the pack. Ashleigh knew the mare wasn't a racehorse, but in her mind, Stardust responded to her slightest cue, galloping down to the wire to thunderous applause.

"Ashleigh, you should get in here and help fold laundry. Half of this stuff is yours."

She jumped at the sound of Caroline's voice and looked around. Her sister was standing in the doorway, holding up a wrinkled T-shirt as though it were a dead fish.

Ashleigh started to snap back, then caught herself. "Sure thing, Caro," she said, and leaped up from the bed, catching Prince Charming before he tumbled from her lap.

Caroline gave her sister a startled look. "Who are

you?" she demanded. "You look like my sister, but you don't sound like her."

Ashleigh grinned and followed her to the laundry room. "Attitude, Caroline," she said in a sure voice. "Attitude is everything."

Caroline rolled her eyes and threw a pair of underwear at Ashleigh. "You sound like one of those self-help gurus," she said, carefully folding a sweater and putting it on her stack of clothes.

Ashleigh ignored her sister, grabbing her own clothing and stuffing it in a basket. "I'll just take it upstairs like this," she said, racing from the room.

"Hey," Caroline called after her. "You're supposed to fold it, Ash."

"That's okay," Ashleigh shouted back. "It'll just get dirty and wrinkled next time I wear it." She pounded up the stairs with her clothes.

The rain stopped that night. By late the next morning the icy slush had finally melted and the roads were safe enough for the Griffens to go pick up Stardust. While Ashleigh iced Moe's leg, her parents hitched up the two-horse trailer and drove away.

After she finished with Moe's treatment, Ashleigh paced in the barn, waiting for her parents to return.

"If you need something to do," Kurt said as she walked past him for the twelfth time, "you could clean some of this old leather."

Ashleigh walked back to him and took the tangle of straps he held out.

"What's this?" she asked, sorting through the pieces.

"Just an old bridle I was hanging on to," he said.

"Did this belong to your daughter?" Ashleigh got the brow band and cheek straps straightened and glanced up at the stable hand.

"It was mine when I was a kid," he said. "I kept it to give to her. I thought you might like to fix it up for your new horse."

"Thanks," she said softly. "I'll take good care of it."

"I know you will, Ashleigh." He walked away, and Ashleigh sat down in the tack room with a bottle of leather conditioner and some soft rags.

By the time Ashleigh heard the truck pull up the drive, she had the soft leather oiled and polished. She hung the bridle from a peg and dashed from the barn. It seemed to take her father forever to get the trailer parked. As he got out of the truck she climbed on the fender of the trailer and peered into the window, trying to get a glimpse of their new horse.

"Go ahead and let her out, Elaine," Mr. Griffen said to Ashleigh's mother when she came around to the back of the trailer. He looked up at Ashleigh, who was still trying to get a good look at the horse through the smoke-colored Plexiglas window. "She loaded and trailered fine. Now let's see what she thinks of her new home."

So nervous and excited she couldn't stand still, Ashleigh jumped from the trailer and stepped back so that her mother could unload Stardust.

The trailer shook with the horse's movement. Mrs. Griffen disappeared into the trailer. Then slowly the horse's hind legs emerged, one easy step at a time. The mare had a solid chestnut coat that gleamed even in the low winter daylight. Ashleigh gripped her hands together. She wouldn't have to spend months helping this horse recover its health, the way she had with Lightning.

Finally the horse stepped free of the trailer, and Ashleigh held her breath, waiting to see Stardust's face.

When Mrs. Griffen turned the mare to face Ashleigh, her heart caught in her throat. The mare's refined head showed her Thoroughbred blood. She was coppery red with a white star that spread from the center of her dainty forehead until it met an elegant white stripe down her face, punctuated by a jaunty white snip that angled across her delicate nose—the only white on her flawless chestnut coat. Stardust was perfect.

"Oh, Mom," Ashleigh breathed, stepping up to stroke the mare's sleek neck. "Wow, she looks big. How tall is she, Dad?"

Mr. Griffen rubbed his thumb across his chin and cocked his head, eyeing the mare. "I'd say well over fifteen hands. Plenty big for you, Ashleigh."

Suddenly Stardust lifted her head and emitted a heartfelt whinny. She received an answering call from the other side of the barn, where the broodmares were in their paddocks, enjoying their first day out since the rain had started.

Everyone laughed. "She's loud," Ashleigh said, taking the lead from her mother.

Stardust immediately pinned her ears and pulled away, dragging the rope through Ashleigh's hands. Before the mare could escape, Mrs. Griffen caught her by the halter.

"Hey there, girl. Take it easy." Mrs. Griffen smoothed the mare's neck, soothing her with quiet words.

Ashleigh stepped back, surprised. She'd never had a horse respond to her like that before.

"Try again, Ash. Maybe something spooked her. It's a new place, with new smells and noises. She probably just needs to be walked around so she can check it all out."

Ashleigh approached the horse again, a little slower

this time. Mrs. Griffen kept a firm hold on Stardust's halter, and Ashleigh took the lead rope. This time the mare swiveled her ears back and forth, as though deciding whether she was going to pin them or not. Finally she settled on halfway back.

"She looks nervous," Ashleigh said, keeping one hand firmly on the lead rope while she reached up with the other to stroke Stardust's nose. The mare pinned her ears again and raised her head out of Ashleigh's reach.

"What's she doing?" Ashleigh said. "I'm not going to hit her. I just want to give her a pat."

Mrs. Griffen frowned, then took the lead from Ashleigh's hand. "Let me try," she said. As soon as Ashleigh stepped away from the mare, Stardust's head relaxed and her ears shifted forward. She allowed Mrs. Griffen to stroke her nose. "I don't know," Ashleigh's mom said. "This is odd. She was a perfect lady when we checked her over at the other farm. Her ground manners were excellent, and your dad and I both rode her without any problems. Try again, sweetheart."

When Ashleigh reached for the mare a third time, Stardust sidestepped, trying to get away. It was so frustrating, Ashleigh wanted to cry.

"I would never do anything to hurt you," she said softly to the mare, trying to soothe her. Stardust flicked her ears, keeping an eye on Ashleigh, who reached slowly for the lead rope, a little less sure of her ability to handle the horse. This time Stardust appeared less flighty. Her head came down and she gave a long, deep snort, as if she'd been holding her breath.

Mrs. Griffen released her hold on the mare. "Walk her off, Ashleigh," she said. "I'll stay right beside you for a while." The mare seemed unwilling to follow, but finally she obeyed the tug on her lead rope and followed Ashleigh. Once the horse seemed to accept Ashleigh's control of the lead rope, Mrs. Griffen walked over to Ashleigh's father. Together they watched Ashleigh lead the mare in circles.

Every time she glanced at the mare, Stardust pulled away and pinned her ears. "What's wrong with her?" Ashleigh turned to her parents. "She hates me."

Both Mr. and Mrs. Griffen had puzzled looks on their faces.

"Just give her time, Ashleigh," Mr. Griffen said. "This is all new to her. She's been out to pasture for almost a year. You're going to have to be patient with her."

"What should I do with her?" Ashleigh asked. She didn't feel very comfortable having Stardust on the lead. What if the mare decided to bolt again or, worse, came after her? Ashleigh had been confident she could handle any horse, at least on the ground. She was shaken by the mare's instant dislike of her.

"Put her inside for tonight," Mr. Griffen said. "We'll be bringing the other horses in soon. Maybe she'll relax once she sees them."

Ashleigh doubted it would make any difference. It wasn't being in a new place that had Stardust so upset. It was Ashleigh.

Ashleigh walked slowly into the barn, Stardust plodding sullenly behind her. "No wonder they gave you away," Ashleigh said to the mare as she opened her stall door. "You're nothing but a big grouch."

She reached up to unbuckle Stardust's halter. The horse raised her head, forcing Ashleigh to stand on tip-toe to reach the buckle. Ashleigh slipped out the stall door and latched it shut, then turned to face Stardust again.

"You're supposed to be my horse, you know," she said. "Well, sort of, anyway. And even if you're not friendly to me, I promise I'll be very good to you. I'll feed you well and give you lots of attention. I've even given you a pretty name—Stardust." Stardust seemed to be listening. Ashleigh reached up to stroke the mare's nose one more time, but as soon as she raised her hand, Stardust turned her back, presenting her round chestnut rump to the stall door. Ashleigh walked away, wondering if Stardust was ever going to trust her.

She wanted to call Mona and tell her about Stardust, but first she had to take care of Moe's leg. Besides, it was sort of embarrassing that the mare had rejected her so completely. Mona would want to come and meet Stardust. Then it hit Ashleigh. When she had seen Frisky for the first time, Ashleigh had ridden her. But Stardust would hardly even let Ashleigh lead her around. Ashleigh didn't know if she dared get on Stardust's back.

Ashleigh knelt in the bedding in Moe's stall, absently stroking his shoulder while his leg soaked. All she could think about was what a bad start she'd had with Stardust.

She glanced up when her father propped his forearms on top of the stall door. "How's the little guy doing?"

Ashleigh looked over at the pony, who seemed content to be in the stall. She and Rory were lavishing attention on him, he was being fed well, and he didn't have to work. "He seems to be pretty good. He isn't favoring the leg anymore, and his cuts are almost healed."

"Good," her father said. "Your face looks a lot better, too."

"Well, thanks a lot, Dad," Ashleigh teased.

"I didn't mean it like that," her father said. "It won't be very noticeable when school starts."

Ashleigh didn't care about her face, but she didn't want to explain to the other kids how she got the scratches. She just wanted to put the whole horrible episode behind her. Knowing Moe's leg was improving would help, too.

"Dr. Frankel will be here tomorrow," her father said. "He can check Stardust over after he's done with Moe and the broodmares."

"Dad, about Stardust . . . do you think she knows somehow that I hurt Moe, and that's why she doesn't trust me?"

"No, Ashleigh, not at all. You're a very capable horse person. While you were putting her in her stall, I called the folks who gave her to us. Stardust has good reason to be afraid."

"But she wasn't afraid of you or Mom. Why me?" Ashleigh lifted Moe's leg from the ice bucket, dried it with a towel, and started wrapping the sturdy bandage around his leg.

"Her owners gave Stardust away when their daughter first left for college, to a girl about your age. Unfortunately, she was working with a trainer who felt the best way to get a horse to cooperate was to use

87

a whip." Her father opened the door to Moe's stall, and Ashleigh carried out the bucket and first aid supplies.

Ashleigh's stomach dropped. "So Stardust and Lightning got abused in the same way."

"Yes, but not for very long. Stardust's owners soon got wise to what was going on and took her back. They feel the same way we do about using a whip to communicate with your horse. We don't get spanked at school when we don't understand something, and we don't whip the horses when they don't understand what we're teaching them. If a horse doesn't get something, we need to try another way of communicating."

Ashleigh nodded. It was something she'd heard many times. "But I wasn't carrying a whip," she protested.

"Yes, but after her bad experience, Stardust must associate the whip with a girl about your height and size. Don't forget that Lightning never fully trusted Kurt or me," her father reminded her. "She remembered that it was a man who had abused her. Horses have very long memories. You know that, Ash. If something hurt or frightened a horse once, the animal always seems to remember it."

Ashleigh nodded, thinking of some of the racehorses she'd heard about who'd had bad experiences on the track. Some of the best runners never recovered mentally. It didn't take a physical injury to end a horse's racing career.

"So what can I do to help Stardust, Dad?"

"A few months before we bought Edgardale," her father said, "your mother and I attended some horse training clinics. One of the trainers relied on a round pen to work with untrained or difficult horses. A round pen is little circular ring with high sides and no corners for the horse to hide in. This trainer did some really amazing things in a very short time."

"So why don't you have a round pen here?" Ashleigh demanded.

"It isn't something we've needed," Mr. Griffen replied. "We can manage the foals with the facilities we have, so putting up a round pen is an expense we couldn't really justify. If we had a training facility, we'd definitely install one."

"How does that help me with Stardust?" Ashleigh asked. "We don't have a round pen, and I don't know how to use one, anyway."

"I'll help you," her father promised. "We can use one of the small paddocks. It doesn't have to be a perfect circle to work. It just needs to keep the horse about as close to you as a longe line would."

After her father left to go back to the house, Ashleigh put away the medical supplies and walked by

Stardust's stall. The mare pinned her ears and narrowed her eyes. Stardust looked almost comical. She couldn't possibly hate Ashleigh that much—they barely even knew each other.

But having talked to her father, Ashleigh felt much more hopeful about Stardust. She eyed Stardust determinedly as the mare paced her new stall. "You're not going to intimidate me, you know. We're going to become friends," she told the mare. Before Stardust could turn her back again, Ashleigh hurried from the barn and rushed up to the house to call Mona.

"She's here," Ashleigh announced matter-of-factly into the phone. She dug an apple from the fruit bowl on the table and began polishing it on her shirt.

"You don't sound very excited," Mona answered tentatively.

"I am," Ashleigh said quickly. "It's just that she needs some work."

Mona gave a shocked gasp. "You mean like Lightning?"

"Well, she's really healthy and fit," Ashleigh explained, taking a bite of the apple. "But she's sort of like Lightning, because she's been abused. She's afraid of me because I look like a girl who used to hit her. I guess she thinks I'm mean, too." Despite having felt hopeful earlier, after her talk with her dad, Ashleigh couldn't help sounding despondent now, saying it all to Mona.

"Boy, that's tough," Mona said sympathetically.

"I know." Ashleigh sighed. "Do you want to help me start training her? My dad has some ideas about how to help her."

"Sure." Mona paused. "But can't we go for a ride right away? I was really looking forward to riding together on our new horses."

"We probably can," Ashleigh said. "She's very well trained. And she can't bite me or get away from me if I'm on her back. Let's go tomorrow after school."

"Great," Mona said. "I'll see you on the bus."

Ashleigh hung up, wondering if riding the mare right away was such a good idea. Her parents had both ridden Stardust, but Ashleigh still didn't feel too sure of herself around the mare.

She took another bite of apple and looked out the window at the gathering dusk. *I'll ride tomorrow,* Ashleigh told herself firmly. She didn't want Mona thinking she was scared of Stardust. She wasn't. It was Stardust who was scared of her. "I'm not afraid of Stardust," she said out loud to the empty kitchen. She wasn't afraid . . . was she?

Christmas break was over, and the first day back at school dragged. When lunchtime finally arrived, Ashleigh hurried to the cafeteria. She found Mona at a table with Lynne and Jamie.

"Congratulations on your horse, Ashleigh," Lynne said. "Maybe I'll get a real horse next."

"Lance is big for a Welsh pony," Ashleigh reminded her. "You won't outgrow him for a long time."

Lynne wrinkled her nose. "You sound like my parents. I keep hoping I'll have a sudden growth spurt."

The girls laughed.

"Tell us about Stardust, Ashleigh," Lynne said, and Ashleigh described her new horse to her friends, leaving out the bad parts.

"She sounds nice," Jamie said, stuffing her empty wrappings into her lunch bag. "Are you going to ride her this afternoon? It's supposed to start raining again tomorrow."

"Yes. Mona's bringing Frisky over so we can introduce her to Stardust."

Ashleigh's parents had agreed to let her try out Stardust with Mona as long as they stayed inside a paddock. Her father thought it might be better to wait and work with the horse on the ground for a few days, but it had been so long since Ashleigh had been able to ride that she begged until they finally gave in.

After school Ashleigh raced up to the house to change her clothes, then hurried to the barn. Rory met her in the aisle. "You get to help me start riding Moe," he said, jumping up and down in the middle of the aisle. "Dr. Frankel said he's okay now."

"That's great, Rory." Ashleigh hurried down the aisle with Rory on her heels.

"I want to ride now," Rory said, following her to Stardust's stall.

"Not now," Ashleigh said. "I have chores to do, then I'm going to ride Stardust."

"No fair," Rory protested. "You got Moe hurt and I couldn't ride him, and now you're too busy to help me. You promised, Ashleigh."

Stardust watched them with an indifferent look in her eyes. Ashleigh glanced at her little brother, whose lower lip was starting to quiver. She looked back at the mare and shrugged. "Okay, I'll help you with Moe, but only for a few minutes. I really want to try out Stardust. Then this weekend maybe we can go for a ride together."

Satisfied, Rory took off for Moe's stall. Ashleigh rushed through her chores, watching the sky through the open barn door. The clouds hung low over the farm, but with any luck the rain would hold off until dark.

Rory had Moe brushed and ready for his tack by the time Ashleigh finished cleaning her assigned stalls. The broodmares and weanlings were inside already, waiting for their dinner.

Ashleigh saddled Moe and helped Rory take him outside. After just a few minutes of walking along the drive, she headed them back to the barn, ignoring Rory's complaints.

"He's only supposed to walk a little bit. You don't want to stress Moe's leg, do you?" She ignored the twinge of guilt she felt when Rory jumped down from the pony's back.

"No way," he said.

Ashleigh helped Rory untack Moe, leaving her brother to groom him, as the pony scrounged bits of leftover hay from the ground beneath his hay net.

Ashleigh dashed to the tack room to grab a saddle and the bridle Kurt had given her. She hurried to Stardust's stall with a carrot. The mare eyed the treat, and rather than turning her back, she approached the door with her ears pricked. Ashleigh broke a piece off the carrot and fed it to her. The mare let Ashleigh stroke her nose, and Ashleigh felt a rush of relief. *Maybe yesterday was just a bad day for Stardust. Today she seems much friendlier.*

Ashleigh slipped the mare's halter on and led her out of the stall. Stardust dragged at the lead rope, and Ashleigh tensed, bracing herself in case the horse decided to bolt, but Stardust didn't try to get away this time. Ashleigh clipped the crossties to her halter and stroked the mare's sleek chestnut neck. "You are going to be my friend, aren't you?" she said. Stardust leaned away from Ashleigh's hand and stamped her foot.

Making friends with this horse is going to be a big job, Ashleigh realized, quickly rubbing her over with a currycomb. *At least she didn't try to kick,* she thought, moving past the mare's tail and to the other side.

Mona would be there soon. Ashleigh had to hurry if they were going to ride. She set the saddle on Stardust's back. The mare tensed and pinned her ears, swinging her head around. Ashleigh was close enough to her shoulder that Stardust couldn't reach her, but Ashleigh heard the snap as the horse's teeth closed together. She jumped back.

"You tried to bite me!" She stared at the unhappy mare for a moment. Now what was she supposed to do? Ashleigh had been so surprised by Stardust's attack that she hadn't moved fast enough to punish the horse immediately. She pointed a finger at the mare and stamped her foot. Stardust jerked her head up and brought her ears forward.

"Next time I'll be ready for you," Ashleigh warned. "I would never whip you, but I won't let you get me, either. You can't go around biting people."

Ashleigh quickly adjusted the saddle and tightened the girth. She unhooked the crossties and slipped the reins over Stardust's head. The mare accepted the bit dutifully, with only one attempt to pull her head away while Ashleigh was slipping the headstall over her ears.

Ashleigh grasped the reins and stepped back. With her gleaming coat and balanced conformation, Stardust looked like her dream horse. Her perfectly shaped head was up and her ears were alert. She was so pretty. Ashleigh sighed. If only Stardust would let Ashleigh be her friend. Now that she was all tacked up, Stardust *looked* ready to be ridden, but Ashleigh wasn't sure she could ride her.

She heard hoofbeats coming up the drive, so she led Stardust outside to meet Mona and Frisky.

Frisky pranced up the driveway, her graceful neck arched as she stepped out elegantly. Ashleigh could imagine how the lively bay mare would have looked on the track, dancing along beside the pony horse as she was led to the starting gate. Her jockey would have been crouched over her withers, balancing on short stirrups, bright silks shining in the sun. Maybe with the right jockey Frisky would have been a great racehorse. Someday, Ashleigh promised herself, she'd be the right jockey for a lot of racehorses. She'd always ride winners.

Mona's beautiful bay mare obeyed her rider instantly, listening attentively for Mona's cues. Ashleigh felt a familiar ache. She would have given a lot to have a well-trained Thoroughbred like Frisky.

She glanced back at Stardust, who had her ears partway back and her hind leg cocked. Compared to Frisky, Stardust looked dumpy and sullen. Ashleigh sighed. Her parents had found her a horse. She should be happy and grateful, not pouting like some spoiled brat. She forced a smile to her face and waved a greeting to Mona.

Mona hopped off Frisky. "So this is Stardust," she said. "She's cute, Ashleigh."

97

Stardust pricked her ears forward when she smelled Frisky. The two mares touched noses. Then Stardust squealed and struck at the ground, her hoof just barely missing Frisky's foreleg. Mona quickly moved her mare away. "And grumpy," Mona added.

Ashleigh shrugged. "I guess all mares can be moody. Anyway, even if our horses don't always get along, when we're riding they'll be listening to us, not paying attention to each other," she added breezily.

"Have you been on her yet?" Mona kept Frisky a safe distance from Stardust's teeth and hooves. Ashleigh didn't blame her. She'd rather be farther away from the cranky mare, too.

But once she got up on Stardust's back, everything would be fine, Ashleigh told herself. She was a good rider. Maybe once her parents saw how well she handled Stardust, they'd let her start exercising the broodmares sometimes, too.

"I'm going to take her into the paddock and try her out right now," Ashleigh told Mona. "I hope you don't mind if we stick to the fenced pasture for today. I need to wait until I get to know her before I take her very far."

"Of course," Mona said. "I felt the same way about Frisky. But she's so attentive, it didn't take long for me to feel confident. I'm sure Stardust will be the same way. Didn't you say she's had a lot of training?"

Ashleigh nodded, leading the way to the paddock. "But not all of it was the right kind," she reminded Mona, shutting the gate behind Stardust. She held the right rein short as she checked Stardust's girth, in case the mare tried to swing around and bite her again. But Stardust stood still, and the saddle felt snug on her back.

Ashleigh dropped the stirrup and put her foot in the iron. As she started to pull herself into the saddle, Stardust suddenly seemed to wake up. She leaped sideways, and Ashleigh, who was only halfway in the saddle, flew off, landing on her side in the muddy paddock.

She lay in the dirt for a second, stunned by how quickly everything had happened. Then she scrambled to her feet and glared at Stardust, who stood a few feet away, watching her.

"Are you okay?" Mona had mounted Frisky again and sat outside the paddock fence, a worried frown on her face.

Ashleigh looked down at her filthy clothes and gritted her teeth. "I'm fine," she said, glaring up at Stardust. "She just caught me by surprise."

"Do you want me to hold her head?" Mona offered as Ashleigh walked to the mare and picked up the reins.

"No, thanks." Ashleigh was determined to get on the horse on her own. She tried to wipe her hands clean on her equally muddy jeans. After a minute she gave up and led Stardust to the side of the paddock, positioning her right side against the fence. "Now she won't be able to go sideways," she said.

She gathered the reins again and tested the stirrup by pulling down on it. Stardust stood stock still. Once again Ashleigh slipped her foot into the iron and swung up, this time trying to be prepared for any surprises Stardust might have. Stardust stood motionless. "Made it," Ashleigh started to say as her seat touched the saddle. But before she could get her foot in the other stirrup, Stardust shot forward. The reins slipped from Ashleigh's mud-slick hand, and she flew off over Stardust's hindquarters, landing on her back in the slop.

Ashleigh stared up at the black clouds overhead. The ground was so soft that she hadn't been hurt when she landed, but she could feel the mud squishing up under her helmet. The sound of laughter made her grind her teeth, and she felt her mood grow blacker than the clouds in the sky. She sat up and glowered at Mona, who clung to Frisky's back, doubled over with laughter.

"I'm sorry, Ash! I can't help laughing. You should have seen it! What an amazing fall!"

Ashleigh jumped to her feet, and exploded before she could stop herself. "Shut up, Mona. Just shut up!" Globs of mud dropped from her jacket and jeans. Ashleigh's anger was mounting by the second, her new positive attitude replaced by humiliation. Ashleigh didn't care about having a good attitude anymore. All it had gotten her was a horse that had dumped her on the ground. Twice.

Mona stopped laughing and sat straight in the saddle, eyes wide. "Look, Ash, I offered to hold her for you, remember? Just because you're a good rider doesn't mean you can just hop on anything and gallop off. I guess Stardust is trying to teach you something."

"Oh Mona, now that you have Frisky you just think you're so great!" Ashleigh yelled in frustration.

Mona bit her lip and started to turn Frisky away. "I'd rather ride alone than with you any day," she said, sounding like she was about to cry. Mona squeezed Frisky into a trot and headed back toward home.

"Fine," Ashleigh called to Mona's rigid back. Her fists were clenched at her sides, and her teeth were gritted so tightly that they hurt. Stardust stood by the paddock fence, idly nibbling at the grass.

"What's going on out here?" Ashleigh's father stood framed in the doorway of the barn.

"I think that horse hates me, Dad," Ashleigh explained, gesturing at Stardust. "She doesn't want me to ride her."

Mr. Griffen walked up to the fence and leaned his forearms on the top rail. When he did, Stardust walked up to him and nudged him like the docile, friendly riding horse she was meant to be. Ashleigh could have screamed. Mr. Griffen grabbed her reins and walked her over to the gate so that he could let himself into the paddock.

"I tried to tell you last night, Ashleigh. You need to slow down and work with her one step at a time. If she doesn't trust you on the ground, what makes you think you can gain her trust while you're on her back?"

"But what if she never trusts me?" Ashleigh felt her lip start to quiver. She wanted to sit down in the middle of the muddy paddock and cry. It was all she could do to keep herself from bursting into racking sobs. "She's like a bucking bronco."

At the look on her father's face, Ashleigh instantly regretted her words. He looked as if he was about to lose patience with her any minute.

"I'm sorry," Ashleigh said. "I didn't mean it. I know she's not that bad."

"You need to start slowly," her father repeated. "I know Stardust is a good horse. I rode her. I wouldn't put you on a horse that wasn't safe, Ashleigh. Right now, though, Stardust doesn't know that you're safe for her." Several fat drops of rain plopped onto Ashleigh's helmet. Some hit her face, mingling with the tears of frustration and the streaks of mud running down her cheeks.

Mr. Griffen undid Stardust's girth, readjusted the saddle pad where it had slipped, and tightened the girth back up again. Ashleigh pressed her lips together as she watched. "It will work out, Ashleigh," her father said as he worked. "You just need to have some patience. Trust me, okay?"

Ashleigh couldn't say anything. She looked down at the mud and nodded tiredly.

"Now, so that she doesn't think she can just throw you and get away with it, I'm going to help you onto the saddle." Mr. Griffen glanced down at Ashleigh's mud-caked jeans and grinned at her. "It's going to need a good cleaning afterward. Starting tomorrow we'll begin the round-pen work I was talking about. If you work with her, not against her, Stardust will end up being a good horse for you, Ashleigh. Promise."

Without a word, Ashleigh followed her father to where Stardust stood. The rain began falling in earnest, but Mr. Griffen picked up the reins, ignoring the downpour.

Her father held the mare's head and Ashleigh cautiously swung onto the saddle. This time Stardust stood like a statue. Then, with her father at the horse's head, Ashleigh walked the mare around the paddock without any problem.

"That's enough for today," Mr. Griffen said, holding Stardust's head while Ashleigh dismounted. "We're both soaked, and that saddle is going to need a good oiling tonight. Take her in and get her cleaned up and fed. But don't spend all day in there—you still have homework to do, remember?"

Ashleigh led Stardust back to her stall, feeling as though a ton of bricks were resting on her shoulders. She didn't know if Stardust would ever grow to trust her. It was going to take a lot of work. But after Lightning, Ashleigh was tired of having to work so hard. She didn't want to fix anyone else's horse. She just wanted to get on and gallop—fast. Maybe Stardust did have it in her to be good. The only hope Ashleigh had to go on was that when her father was there, Stardust behaved perfectly. But she had to learn to act that way for Ashleigh, too. Ashleigh pulled off the saddle and began rubbing Stardust with a thick towel.

"You and I are going to become friends," she said, as if telling the troubled mare would make it so.

Stardust lowered her delicate head to make it easier for Ashleigh to rub her crest with the towel. For once the mare seemed to let her guard down, and she snorted contentedly. Ashleigh felt a glimmer of hope. Maybe she and Stardust could really work things out. Ashleigh hoped so with all her heart. She had wished on a star for this horse—she couldn't just give up on her.

8

"Ashleigh, wait up!"

Ashleigh stopped, letting the rush of students flow past her in the school hallway as she waited for Lynne. When the other girl reached her, they followed the stream of students heading for the cafeteria.

Lynne watched the students lining up for hot lunch and cringed. "I'm glad my mom has time to pack my food," she said. "I don't think eating lunchroom surprise every day would be much fun."

"Me too," Ashleigh said, inhaling deeply. "It smells like the midweek mystery meat stew. Everything leftover from Monday and Tuesday."

The girls burst into giggles and hurried to find an empty table as more students filed into the noisy room. They settled down with their lunches and began to eat their sandwiches. Lynne leaned forward, raising her voice to be heard over the cafeteria clamor.

"I'm having a 'Day at the Races' party tomorrow after school. Can you come? My mom says January is always such a long, boring month. She wanted to do something fun."

"What races?" Ashleigh perked up at the idea of a horse racing party to liven up the first week back at school.

"You know that sports channel that shows a bunch of horse races? Tomorrow they're going to have the Gulfstream races on. My mom said she'd make Triple Crown nachos and infield punch, and a winner's circle cake."

"Wanderer's Quest is in Florida," Ashleigh said, her interest piqued. "I wonder if she's going to be running in any races tomorrow. It would be great to see her run." Wanderer's Quest was the just turned four-year-old mare out of the Griffens' best broodmare, Wanderer. Quest had already won her share of races for her owners, the Fontaines, and was gradually moving up the ranks. Thanks to her, Edgardale was making a name for itself among Thoroughbred breeders.

"What time is the party?" Ashleigh asked. "I know my mom will say yes."

Some other students joined them at the table, and they talked about the party for several minutes. It wasn't until Ashleigh rose to leave that she realized she hadn't seen Mona since the bus ride that morning. Mona had taken a seat well away from Ashleigh, keeping her back turned for the whole ride.

When she glanced around the cafeteria, Ashleigh spotted Mona at another table with several kids Ashleigh barely knew.

Fine, she thought. Mona hadn't been acting like much of a friend anyway, telling her she wasn't a very good rider just because Stardust acted up. If Mona was going to ignore her, Ashleigh would ignore Mona right back.

Mona's mom must have picked her up after school, because Ashleigh didn't see her on the bus. The rain that had started the night before was still falling when the driver dropped Ashleigh at the end of the Griffens' drive. She pulled her hood over her head and dashed up the drive to the house, quickly changed her clothes, and hurried to the barn.

When she went to the isolation stall to check on Moe, it was empty.

"Dad? Mom?" Ashleigh hurried through the barn to Moe's regular stall. The pony stood inside, dozing.

Ashleigh jogged down the aisle to her parents'

office. Her father sat at the desk tapping numbers into a calculator.

"You moved Moe. Does that mean he's all better? I know Dr. Frankel said Rory could ride him lightly, but what about the ice treatments?"

"The vet said no more ice baths," her father said. "Just keep light support on that leg, and remember to use the sports boots when you have Rory ride him."

Rain thundered on the barn roof, and her father glanced out the office's small window. The water sheeted down the glass, blurring the view outside. "Nasty weather," he said.

"I guess we won't be working Stardust in the round pen today," Ashleigh said, disappointed. "I'm going to groom her in her stall after I've done my chores. If you need me, that's where I'll be."

"All right." Her father hit a button on the calculator and glanced back up at her. "But I've been thinking, Ashleigh. Since you need to gain her trust, from now on you'll have the full responsibility of feeding her morning and night. That should help her bond to you. The girl who had her kept her at a stable, where it was adults who fed and cared for her."

"No wonder she doesn't have any good feelings toward me," Ashleigh said. Now that she was beginning to understand why Stardust acted the way she did, Ashleigh had stopped feeling so angry and had started feeling sorry for the mare.

Ashleigh rushed through her chores, eager to spend time with Stardust so that they could start to form some sort of bond. Now that she didn't have to baby-sit Moe for hours every day while his leg soaked, she had plenty of time to spend working with the mare.

Stardust seemed to settle down once Ashleigh started brushing her. "We're going to be best friends, Stardust," she said, rubbing the mare's shoulder with the soft rubber comb. Stardust stood quietly while Ashleigh combed her mane. "We're going to have such great adventures," Ashleigh promised the horse. "I want to learn to be a jockey and race like the wind. Since you have some Thoroughbred in you, I hope you like to run, too. That's what I like best. Someday I'm going to have my own Thoroughbred training farm. I'll only have the best racehorses." She glanced at the mare quickly, realizing what she had said didn't sound very nice. Ashleigh patted Stardust's coppery neck. "But there'll be a place for you, too," Ashleigh added.

She fed the mare according to her father's directions, giving her only a tiny bit of grain along with a netful of hay. Then she hurried up to the house for dinner.

"Have you talked to Mona lately?" her mother asked while they were at the table.

"No," Ashleigh said, not wanting to bring up the subject of Mona.

"I just wondered how she was doing with her new mare," Mrs. Griffen said, ladling sauce onto her plate of spaghetti.

"Fine, I guess," Ashleigh replied. Eager to change the subject, she told her parents about Lynne's "Day at the Races" party. As she was talking she wondered if Mona was going to be there, too. She hoped Mona wouldn't spend the whole afternoon making a point of ignoring her. That would just ruin the party.

After dinner she hurried to get her homework done before bedtime. Now that she was making progress with Stardust—at least Stardust was letting Ashleigh brush her ears and move around her without trying to bite her—Ashleigh had to be careful to keep her grades up so that her parents wouldn't take the horse away from her.

When Ashleigh rang the Durans' doorbell the next afternoon, the bell chimed the call to the post, like in the races. Lynne's mother opened the door, giggling at the silly chime, and gestured for Ashleigh to come in. Ashleigh hurried into the house out of the rain. "Take off that rain slicker and leave it right here," Mrs.

Duran said, pointing at a rack laden with damp coats. "The other kids are in the family room."

Like many families in the area, the Durans were horse people. The house was decorated with racing memorabilia and the walls had framed prints of Lynne riding in shows. In the entryway was a rug with the image of a running horse embossed on its surface.

A large banner reading "Triple Crown Club— Members Only" hung over the entry to the family room. Ashleigh hurried inside, eager to join the party. The big-screen television was already showing the prerace activities at the Gulfstream track.

"Guess what, Ash?" Lynne greeted her with an excited wave. "I found out Wanderer's Quest *is* running. I can't wait."

"Great!" Ashleigh exclaimed in delight. She had been so busy with Moe and now Stardust that she hadn't paid much attention to the track schedules. Ashleigh grabbed a handful of popcorn and quickly settled in with the group.

"Did you invite Mona?" she asked Lynne, who was pouring punch into plastic cups. Lynne looked uncomfortable at the question.

"Did you?" Ashleigh repeated.

"She said she wouldn't come if you were here," Lynne finally said. "I told her I wasn't going to uninvite you but that she was still welcome to come. I didn't know you guys were mad at each other."

Ashleigh fought off a shadow of guilt. She had been mean to Mona, but Mona hadn't exactly been nice to her, either. "Oh, well," Ashleigh said with a shrug. "I guess it's up to her. But I wouldn't have minded if she was here."

Ashleigh was distracted by the voice of the announcer as he gave the post positions for the first race. Lynne's mom had taped a big sheet of paper to the wall so that everyone could put their name by their favorite horse in each race.

"I want the number four horse in race one," Jamie said, balancing a cup of punch and a plate of food while she scribbled her name on the paper.

"Why?" Ashleigh asked, looking at the list of horses scheduled for the race.

Jamie raised her eyebrows and grinned. "I like the name. Sheeza Juan."

Ashleigh groaned. "What if the same horse had a name like Slowpoke?"

"Then I'd pick a different horse," Jamie said. "I think they live up to their names."

The first race was a six-and-a-half-furlong claiming race for two-year-old fillies. Based on the odds and the number of wins the horse had had that season,

Ashleigh picked her favorite from the field of eight, a filly called On a Wing, and found a place to sit in front of the television. She propped her plate of cheese-laden nachos on her knees.

When the horses broke from the gate, the room filled with voices urging the Thoroughbreds on.

"Oh, look at them go! Come on, Sheeza!"

Ashleigh tore her eyes from the screen to glance at Jamie, who had her fists clenched, her attention riveted to the television. Jamie's pick had broken badly from the gate and was lying in tenth place. Then she looked back at the screen and forgot Jamie. Her own pick, the number seven horse, was in third place and moving up fast.

"Come on, On a Wing," she called, leaning forward as if she were riding the filly herself. Then the jockey reached back with his whip to tap the horse's rump. "Don't!" Ashleigh yelled, as if the jockey could hear her. "She's doing her best!" The filly caught up with the second-place horse, but then they were under the wire. When the numbers came up, Ashleigh's horse had only placed third.

Ashleigh sighed. "He distracted her when he got her with the whip," she said, sitting back with a scowl.

"Oh, right, Ash, blame the jockey," Lynne teased, although she had nothing to boast about. Lynne's horse had come in second to last, just ahead of Jamie's.

Wanderer's Quest was running in the fourth race, an ungraded stakes race for fillies and mares three and up. Ashleigh didn't care about the performance of the rest of the field. She quickly put her name by the mare's position number and waited tensely for the race to begin.

When the horses broke from the gate, she strained to keep track of Quest. But in the number four position, she was hard to pick from the crush of horses charging around the track.

"Where is she, Ash? Do you see her?" Lynne sat beside her, her eyes, like Ashleigh's, glued to the television.

The announcer's voice rose as the horses passed the first pole. "It's Run Lady Run in the lead, with Flatiron coming up on the inside. The rest of the pack is tightly bunched, but it looks like Wanderer's Quest fighting with True Heart for third. Look at that black mare go!"

Ashleigh squeezed her fists and pumped her elbows, feeling her heart thunder in her chest as though she was running the race right along with Wanderer's Quest. The whole room gasped as Quest put on a burst of speed at the half-mile marker to surge up past True Heart in third.

"Too soon," she groaned. "Don't make her push the

leaders too soon." As if he heard her, the jockey checked Quest, keeping her in a strong third place. As they approached the sixteenth pole the rider leaned forward, letting Quest fly past the leaders to cross the finish line with a lead of half a length.

Ashleigh leaped from the floor, whooping and clapping her hands overhead. "We did it! She won!"

"Congratulations, Ash!"

"What a great race!"

"It's so cool that you helped raise her!"

The rest of the party passed in a blur of races and lots of joking about how to pick winners. By the time Mrs. Griffen picked Ashleigh up that evening, she was tired but elated. An Edgardale horse had won another race.

"Quest ran such a great race," Ashleigh told her mother, bouncing into the car.

Mrs. Griffen backed the car out of the Durans' driveway, smiling. "I know, I listened to it on the radio. Incredible," she agreed. "I'm sure the Fontaines are thrilled. Let's hope Tonka does as well next year."

"And Wanderer's next foal, of course," Ashleigh added.

"And Slewette's foals, and Jolita's foals—"

"And all the Edgardale foals," Ashleigh exclaimed, laughing.

"Don't forget," her mother reminded her, bringing

her back to practical reality, "you still need to get your homework done tonight."

"I know," Ashleigh sighed, glad she hadn't been assigned a lot of math homework so far this week. She and Mona usually did their math together. Ashleigh's heart sank when she thought of all the fights she and Mona had been having. Mona would have been thrilled by Quest's win, but because of Ashleigh she hadn't even come to Lynne's party. Ashleigh knew one of them would have to apologize, but it was Mona's turn this time.

"According to the forecast, the weather is supposed to break tomorrow. Maybe then you and your father can start working with Stardust." Mrs. Griffen patted a pile of books and videotapes on the seat beside her, interrupting Ashleigh's thoughts. "I stopped by the library and picked up some information on round-pen training. The tapes are by the same trainer who put on the clinic your dad and I attended. They might help you in dealing with Stardust's behavior."

"Thanks, Mom." Ashleigh picked up one of the books and flipped through it, her attention gripped by the photos she saw scattered through the pages. All thoughts of Mona flew out of her head as she became absorbed by what she saw. Here was hope for her and Stardust.

That night Ashleigh went to bed with a flashlight and the round-pen manual, waiting until Caroline was breathing deeply and evenly before she switched on the light and began to read.

When she finally flicked the flashlight off and rested her head on the pillow an hour later, Ashleigh's mind was filled with plans of what she would do with Stardust. Armed with the information in the book, and with her father's help, Ashleigh was going to turn Stardust around—she was sure of it. Mona could help her, too, if the two friends ever made up. But soon Stardust was going to be the best friend Ashleigh ever had.

9

"Good going, Ashleigh." Mr. Griffen stood outside Edgardale's smallest paddock, watching Ashleigh and Stardust. "Now ask her to make another inside turn."

"She's listening to me!" Ashleigh flashed a grin at her father.

"Keep a close eye on her," her father reminded her. Ashleigh quickly fixed her attention back on Stardust, who trotted in a circle around her. The mare was completely bare of any tack, not even a halter. Mr. Griffen had attached sheets of plywood at the corners of the paddock, taking away the sharp angles. Now Stardust didn't have any corners to head into.

After watching her father work the mare in the pen for a short time, Ashleigh had taken over. Studying the books and videos from the library had helped Ashleigh understand the round-pen training methods. It looked as though Stardust was responding, too.

Stardust slowed down to a walk. Ashleigh stayed toward her hindquarters and drove the mare away again, waving her arms. The trick was to keep Stardust moving forward without frightening her. "This is like rubbing my head and patting my stomach at the same time," she called to her father, careful not to take her eyes off the horse again. "I'm glad I read that book on free longeing. It all kind of makes sense now." Ashleigh watched the mare's head position, waiting for Stardust to look toward her as she circled the round pen.

As soon as Stardust looked toward Ashleigh instead of the outside of the pen, Ashleigh stepped back. Stardust turned to her, and Ashleigh moved toward the mare's outside shoulder, using body language to turn the horse and send her moving the other way.

"That's great," Mr. Griffen called. "Now drop your hands and look at the ground."

As soon as Ashleigh did what her father said, Stardust turned and trotted up to her, stopping right in front of Ashleigh. As Ashleigh reached up to rub the mare's forehead, she felt a rush of confidence. She was a good trainer!

Stardust was breathing hard from the effort of trotting in the sloppy paddock. She looked tired. "What if she decides she doesn't like what I'm making her do,

Dad? She's just going to dislike me all that much more."

Ashleigh hadn't worked nearly as hard as Stardust, but she had kept moving, too, chasing the horse around. She felt warm and energized. This would be a perfect day to go for a ride—if only Stardust was ready to ride.

Mr. Griffen walked into the paddock carrying Stardust's halter. "Try to think like the horse, Ashleigh. She understands she has a choice. She can stand with you and get petted when she does what you ask, or if she acts up, you chase her off and she has to work hard."

Ashleigh laughed. "So if she pins her ears at me, I chase her off, right?"

"Exactly. After a while she'll figure out you're going to reward her for good behavior. She'll do whatever you ask."

"I watched part of the video from the library. That trainer really understands horses, doesn't he?"

Mr. Griffen handed Ashleigh Stardust's halter. "He's what they used to call a horse whisperer."

"I don't know why they call it horse whispering," Ashleigh said, petting Stardust's shoulder. "It seems like mostly the training involves listening to the horse, not whispering to it."

"Exactly!" Her father laughed. "You're going to make a great trainer, Ash."

Stardust stood quietly while Ashleigh slipped her halter on.

"Watch this, Dad." Ashleigh draped the lead rope over Stardust's neck and started to walk away without any contact with the horse. The mare followed, keeping her head at Ashleigh's shoulder. "Did you see that?" Ashleigh gasped. "She's doing what I ask, and I don't even have a hand on her!"

"I see," her dad said. "Keep up the good work, sweetheart. You're both doing great."

Ashleigh worked for a while longer with the mare, then spent extra time grooming Stardust before she put her away. "We are going to have such good times," she promised the mare, giving her soft nose a kiss. "Maybe I can even learn to ride you without a bridle. Wouldn't that impress Mona?"

Ashleigh headed for the house to call her friend and tell her about working Stardust in the round pen. She was halfway there before she remembered that she and Mona hadn't spoken since Sunday. Ashleigh slowed to a walk. She missed Mona. But this time, Mona should have called her to apologize. Ashleigh still had other friends, friends who loved horses, but all her big adventures had been with Mona.

Then Ashleigh remembered Kira. It had been a while since she'd spoken to her friend at Hopewell. She wondered how Lightning was doing, too. As soon as Ashleigh had Stardust settled, she ran up to the house.

Ashleigh picked up the phone and dialed Hopewell, asking for Kira after Penny, the supervisor, answered the phone. Kira came to the phone with an excited rush of words. "Ashleigh, I'm going home!"

"Wow! When?" Ashleigh was shocked.

"Day after tomorrow. My doctors in Ohio can keep track of my blood levels, so I don't need to stay at Hopewell anymore. I'm so excited. I can't wait," Kira explained. "My parents are coming down to get me. Can you come over so I can see you before I leave?"

"Definitely. I'll see when Kurt can bring me over," Ashleigh promised.

"Great! I don't want to go without saying good-bye to you. And while you're here you can visit Lightning, too. She'll be so glad to see you again," Kira said.

To her surprise, Ashleigh realized that she hadn't thought much about Lightning the last couple of days. She had been too busy working at winning Stardust over.

"Lightning is really going to miss you, Kira," Ashleigh said, trying to keep the sadness out of her voice. Ashleigh was going to miss Kira a lot, too.

"I know." Kira's voice fell a notch. "I'm going to miss her so much. That's the only bad thing about leaving. But she belongs to Hopewell, and she's very happy here. All the little kids love her. She's so sweet."

Completely the opposite of Stardust, Ashleigh thought. It was going to take her a long time to win Stardust over. But Ashleigh had to console herself with the fact that she and Stardust had already made a lot of progress.

"Ashleigh," Kira said, breaking into her thoughts, "what's happening with you?"

"Well, the big news is, I have a new horse to work with." Ashleigh quickly told Kira all about Stardust.

"Is Mona helping you train her?" Kira asked.

Ashleigh caught her breath. "No," she said awkwardly. "Mona and I aren't talking right now."

"Oh, no," Kira said. "Why not?"

"Well, we had a fight," Ashleigh admitted. She went on to tell Kira everything, beginning with Moe's fall, then Stardust's arrival and Ashleigh's ups and downs with the new mare. Somehow, as she explained things to Kira, Ashleigh couldn't quite put her finger on why she and Mona had been fighting in the first place.

"You need to make up with Mona, Ashleigh," Kira said. "She's your best friend. You guys need each other—you can't just stop speaking. I'm sure Mona would love to help you with Stardust. You were both so excited to have your own horses so that you could ride together, remember?"

"Oh, Kira. You're so patient with people and so nice. How do you do it?" Ashleigh demanded.

"I guess it goes with the cancer. I spend a lot of time with nice doctors," Kira said, then laughed. "I hope that won't go away like the cancer has. I like understanding people. Maybe I'll be a psychologist when I grow up."

After she got off the phone with Kira, Ashleigh wandered into the living room. Caroline was curled up on the sofa, a book in her hand. Rory was in front of the television watching a cartoon.

"You guys are great," Ashleigh said suddenly, surprising even herself.

Caroline looked up in surprise. "You too, Ash. Even if you do keep your half of the room looking like Hurricane Ashleigh has always just blown through, I still love you."

Rory didn't even take his eyes off the television. "I love everyone," he said, petting Prince Charming, who was curled on his lap. "Even your cat, Ashleigh."

Ashleigh took a deep breath, hurried into the kitchen, and picked up the phone. It wouldn't kill her to apologize to Mona first.

She waited, twisting the cord around her wrist,

while Mrs. Gardener called Mona to the phone.

"Hello?"

At the sound of Mona's voice, Ashleigh bit hard on her lower lip. Maybe it wouldn't kill her, but apologizing was still hard.

"I'm sorry, Mona. I was acting kind of mean. I want to make up," Ashleigh said tentatively.

"I'm really sorry, too, Ash," Mona said. She sounded relieved. "We need to quit getting in fights. I'm tired of it."

"Me too," Ashleigh said sincerely. She was glad she had apologized. "Can you come over this weekend and help me work with Stardust? You won't believe how well she's doing."

"What do you mean? What have you guys been up to?"

Ashleigh told her friend all about working with Stardust in the round pen, using her body and her voice to get the mare to listen to and trust her. "She's like a different horse, Mona. You'll see."

"It sounds so great," Mona said. "I can't wait to see how it works. Ash, I have to go. My mom wants me to try on some new clothes she picked up at the mall. She has no clue about what I like." Mona sighed. "If I show up tomorrow in some really dumb-looking outfit, promise me you won't laugh."

Ashleigh thought of her own pile of jeans and wrinkled T-shirts and giggled. "Me, laugh at someone else's clothes? No way, Mona."

"Okay," Mona said, laughing. "I'll see you on the bus tomorrow. We can talk then."

"Bye, Mona." Ashleigh hung up feeling better than she had for days. She and Mona were friends again. Not only that, Stardust was starting to trust her. Ashleigh couldn't wait for the day when she and Stardust and Mona and Frisky could all go out on the trails together.

Saturday morning Mrs. Griffen led Moe out of his stall. "Ashleigh, will you spend a little time helping Rory with Moe before you start working with Stardust?"

Ashleigh started to protest. She wanted to get on with Stardust's training. But her words died on her lips. After all, she had promised to help Rory. "Sure, Mom," she agreed.

She began to groom Moe while Rory finished cleaning his two stalls. Then Rory carried the pony saddle from the tack room, his face bright with excitement.

"Can we canter today, Ashleigh?"

"Not yet. Dr. Frankel said just to walk him for another week." She handed Rory one of Moe's little sports boots, which her allowance had paid for. "We need to put these on him to protect his legs."

Rory seemed content to walk Moe along the lane between the paddocks. Ashleigh trudged beside him, thinking again how fun it would be to finally ride Stardust on the trails.

"Maybe by the time Moe's leg is completely healed," she said, "Stardust will be okay to ride, too. Then we can go on a long ride. Won't that be fun?"

"You'd take me with you?" At the surprised look on Rory's face, Ashleigh laughed.

"Of course we would." Then she remembered how she had felt when she couldn't keep up with Mona and Frisky. "But we'll make sure you set the pace. We don't want to leave Moe behind."

"Thanks, Ash," Rory said, reaching behind him to pat Moe's fuzzy hindquarters.

While Rory brushed his pony down after the short ride, Ashleigh led Stardust into the makeshift round pen. She had just started sending her off to trot around the pen when Mona pedaled up on her bike.

At the sight of the bike, Stardust rolled her eyes and dashed to the far side of the pen.

"Oops." Mona quickly wheeled the bike out of sight and hurried back.

Ashleigh watched the agitated horse with concern.

Stardust was trotting quickly with her head held high, her ears twitching nervously.

When Mona returned, Ashleigh looked at her and shook her head. "That's not a very good sign," she said. "If Stardust is afraid of bikes, what else is going to scare her?"

Mona leaned over the top rail. "I don't know, Ashleigh. I think I just took her by surprise. Maybe she'd be okay if she was with other horses and a bike went by."

"Maybe." Ashleigh hoped Mona was right. Lots of people bicycled along the roads. If every one of them spooked Stardust, she would be a nervous wreck in no time.

"So," Mona said, "show me what you've been doing with her."

Ashleigh quit worrying about the bike for the moment. The trainer on the videotape had gotten a very nervous young horse used to a huge red umbrella. She should be able to help Stardust get used to a bike.

With Mona watching, Ashleigh sent Stardust off again, waving her arms and tossing a bit of dirt in her direction. After a few minutes the mare was following her around the paddock, as if Ashleigh held an invisible lead rope.

"That's cool, Ash." Mona looked impressed.

Ashleigh was pleased. "She's doing great, isn't she?"

"Have you ridden her yet?" Mona asked.

"No." Ashleigh wanted to explain that Stardust wasn't quite ready yet, but she thought it would sound as if she were afraid to ride her. "Let me get a saddle." *We can at least try,* Ashleigh thought. *If Stardust acts up, we might be back at square one. But it's a risk I'll have to take.*

Ashleigh took her time bringing the tack outside. She wasn't afraid, she told herself. She just didn't want to move too fast around Stardust.

When Ashleigh returned to the paddock, she showed off more of Stardust's training, holding her hand out flat to beckon the mare. Stardust came right over.

"Wow," Mona said.

Ashleigh felt bolder, seeing how cooperative Stardust was acting. She set the saddle in place on the mare's back and tightened the girth. Stardust stood still, her ears flicking back and forth.

"You're being such a good girl," Ashleigh crooned, rubbing Stardust's shiny copper-colored shoulder. "What a good girl," she repeated.

"I can't believe this is the same horse that dumped you in the dirt last week," Mona said.

"She isn't," Ashleigh said quickly, wishing Mona hadn't reminded her. It was hard enough dealing with

Stardust without Mona bringing that up. Stardust had come such a long way.

She slipped Stardust's bridle on and pulled the reins over her head.

"Do you want me to hold her head this time?"

Ashleigh gave Mona a quick look. "Sure. I think she'll be good, but it can't hurt."

While Mona slipped into the pen, Ashleigh buckled her helmet. She stood at Stardust's side and waited until Mona had a good hold on the reins.

"Ready when you are," Mona said.

Ashleigh took a deep breath and exhaled. Then, without stopping to think, she swung onto Stardust's back and waited for the explosion.

Stardust stood like a statue. Ashleigh noticed her hand was trembling as she reached down to stroke the horse's neck. She forced herself to relax her legs a little, not wanting to send Stardust forward.

"Ready to walk?" Mona looked up at her and smiled.

Ashleigh gave a brief nod, and Mona led them around the paddock. Stardust kept her head down and her steps steady. After a couple of trips around the paddock, Ashleigh felt more comfortable. "Thanks, Mona," she said, gathering the reins. "I think I'm ready to try her alone now."

Mona released her grip on the bridle and stepped

back, and Ashleigh asked Stardust to walk forward. The mare flexed at the poll and walked off smartly, her neck arched and her carriage perfect.

"Good going," Mona said. "She looks great, Ash. You both do!"

Ashleigh circled the paddock at a walk several times. Feeling brave, she asked Stardust to pick up a trot. The mare perked up and stepped out, and Ashleigh began posting to the rhythmic gait. She asked Stardust to perform a few figure eights. The mare responded to every cue promptly, and Ashleigh felt as though she were on top of the world.

She brought the mare to a stop beside Mona, patted her neck, and jumped off. Mona gave her a high five as she landed.

"I did it!" Ashleigh exclaimed.

Mona was grinning broadly. "Now we can start riding together again. We both have awesome new horses, and we're going to have so much fun. Oh, Ash, this is going to be the best year ever!"

10

Rory sat in Moe's saddle, bouncing with impatience. "Come on, Ashleigh. It's going to get dark soon."

Ashleigh laughed and finished tightening Stardust's girth. "Rory, I know it's winter, but it's still morning. It won't get dark for hours."

"Well, hurry up anyway." Rory laughed.

Ashleigh checked her helmet strap and swung onto the saddle. Stardust stood quietly, waiting for Ashleigh's directions. Ashleigh settled on the mare's back, feeling a broad grin spread across her face. This was it! She was riding Stardust out on the lanes. Ashleigh patted Stardust's smooth neck and gave a contented sigh. Stardust was slowly becoming the horse she had dreamed of owning. Ashleigh had the satisfaction of knowing she was making it happen herself.

"See how well Stardust is going now? I'm going to be a great trainer someday," she said to Rory.

Rory made an impatient sound. "Let's just be great riders for now, okay? I want to go, Ash!"

"Lead the way," she said, picking up the reins. Rory and Moe started down the wide lane between the paddocks. Ashleigh moved Stardust into a walk behind them. The mare walked along slowly, letting Moe set the pace. Following Rory and Moe wasn't exactly what she had in mind for a trail ride. But seeing how soundly Moe was going was such a relief that Ashleigh couldn't be too bothered by the slow pace.

But after a few minutes Ashleigh stifled a yawn of frustration. Plodding along behind the pony made riding incredibly tedious. Since this was the first time she had Stardust out of the paddock, she wanted to try her at a canter down the lane. She took a deep breath and sat back a little. Maybe later she would ride alone. Right now she had promised Rory they would go slow. Moe wasn't ready for more yet.

"This is fun," Rory called over his shoulder. He began weaving Moe from one side of the lane to the other.

Ashleigh swallowed another yawn.

"Come on, Ash! Follow the leader!"

Ashleigh sighed in resignation and asked Stardust to follow Moe's serpentine trail.

"Boring," she muttered, guiding the mare to the left, then the right. *If Mona's free this afternoon, maybe we can take a longer ride,* Ashleigh thought, *without Moe and Rory to slow us down.* She was just dying to try Stardust at a canter outside the paddock. They could go up on the big field at Mona's and practice flying lead changes. And then, once she had a better feel for Stardust out in the open, Ashleigh wanted to gallop.

Ashleigh imagined herself crouched over the mare's muscular shoulders, Stardust's copper-colored mane whipping back in her face. She could hear the drumming of hooves as they raced down the lane, fence posts flashing past, faster and faster—

Suddenly Stardust was flying sideways. Ashleigh grabbed the horse's mane with both hands to keep from sailing out of the saddle. Before she could catch her balance, Stardust jumped forward and crowhopped. They nearly ran Moe over, Stardust's sudden movement throwing Ashleigh forward onto her shoulder. Ashleigh braced herself against the mare's withers and grabbed for the flapping reins.

"Knock it off," Rory yelled, hanging on to Moe's mane as the pony scooted out of Stardust's path.

Just as Ashleigh started to gather the reins, a small gust of wind whipped around them. Before she could balance herself, Stardust gave a loud snort and was out from under her.

Ashleigh flew over the horse's shoulder, keeping a firm hold on the reins. She landed hard on her back, then scrambled to her feet, afraid the agitated mare might trample her.

"Wow," Rory said, his voice awed as he circled Moe back to where Ashleigh stood holding Stardust. "Are you okay, Ash? She really spun around fast."

Ashleigh took a breath and tried to stop her knees from shaking. Stardust stood trembling, her eyes rolling. Her head was up and alert, her neck arched in an exaggerated way. She gave another loud snort.

Ashleigh could see the whites of Stardust's eyes as the horse stared across the pasture in terror. She looked around to see what had startled the mare, but the only things in view were the sweeping pastures and white fences. None of the grazing mares and foals looked concerned. Whatever had set Stardust off had been seen by her alone.

"I think I'm done riding, Rory," Ashleigh said in a quiet voice. She felt a little sick to her stomach, and her nerves were shot. Stardust's sudden bolt had shaken her confidence. "That makes three times you've dumped me," Ashleigh said to the horse through gritted teeth. Riding Stardust didn't seem as though it would ever be very much fun.

She turned around to head back, but after a few

steps she realized that Rory and Moe weren't following.

"Come on, let's go back, Rory." She glanced at her brother, whose jaw was set in a stubborn line.

"No." Rory glared at her. "We didn't go far at all. You've fallen off horses lots of times. Just get back on. That's what Mom and Dad said you're always supposed to do. Ash, you promised we'd get to take a real ride."

Ashleigh blew out an exasperated breath. She'd fallen off Moe lots of times, but she was learning quickly that the ground felt harder when you fell from higher up.

"Later, Rory. Maybe we can ride again later." *But in the paddock,* she thought. Until she knew how to teach Stardust not to spook, she didn't like the idea of going anyplace that wasn't fenced in. Ashleigh wanted to be a jockey, not a crash test dummy for riding helmets.

Rory headed back toward the barn, his little shoulders slumped. Ashleigh started to mount up, but her hands were shaking so badly that she couldn't even get herself into the saddle. Ashleigh felt her own shoulders sag as she lifted the reins over Stardust's head, avoiding the stubborn mare's gaze. Slowly Ashleigh led Stardust back along the lane, weighted down by a sense of defeat.

When they reached the barn, a strange man was standing in the aisle with Ashleigh's parents and Kurt. Ashleigh barely glanced at the older man before she put Stardust in the crossties. Lots of people visited Edgardale to see the Griffens' foals.

But this man didn't look like a buyer. Most of the people who came shopping for horses dressed well. This man wore the same kind of faded jeans and well-worn barn jacket that Kurt always wore. He kept looking at Ashleigh and Stardust and frowning, as though he wanted to talk to her. Ashleigh wondered if he was Stardust's previous owner, checking on his horse. At that moment she didn't care if he took the mare away. Ashleigh had wanted a horse to ride, not one to practice falling off of.

Ashleigh helped Rory with Moe's tack to make up for cutting the ride short. They put the pony in his stall, and Rory stamped up to the house without even thanking her. Ashleigh watched him go and groaned. Couldn't she make it through just one day without getting somebody mad at her?

When she had Stardust untacked, Ashleigh led her to her stall. Kurt and the stranger strolled out of the barn, deep in conversation. Ashleigh's parents walked toward her, frowns on their faces. Ashleigh watched them approach, absentmindedly rubbing Stardust's nose while she waited. The pretty chestnut horse was quiet and friendly again. "Why can't you be this nice when I ride you?" Ashleigh wondered.

Her parents stopped at Stardust's stall, and Mr. Griffen gave the mare a dark look. His furrowed brow and the grim line of his mouth made Ashleigh anxious.

"What's wrong? Is that man here to take Stardust away?"

Her father looked confused for a second. He glanced at the end of the barn where Kurt and the other man had gone, then looked back at Ashleigh.

"No, Ash, it's nothing like that. He's not here about Stardust." Mr. Griffen sighed and looked at Ashleigh's mother as if for help.

"But honey, we do need to talk about Stardust. We think she just isn't working out." Mrs. Griffen said. She put her arms around Ashleigh's shoulders and gave her a gentle squeeze.

"What do you mean?" Ashleigh asked, panic suddenly gripping her. Maybe she was having trouble with the mare, but Stardust was the only horse she had. "She just needs time, right, Dad?"

"We saw what happened out there, Ashleigh," her father said.

Tears welled up in Ashleigh's eyes. "She just spooked a little. I can help her with that." She didn't want her parents to know how much Stardust's spooky behavior had unnerved her. Then she'd never get a second chance.

"We don't want you getting hurt, sweetheart. You handled it well this time and you were lucky, but Stardust needs someone who has a little more experience and can work through her problems."

"I can handle it. I'll be patient," Ashleigh insisted. All of a sudden, keeping Stardust seemed very important. "You can't take her away from me now. I've been working so hard. Can't we please keep her?"

"Ash," her father said firmly, "I saw what she did out on the lane. None of the other horses spooked. Stardust had no reason to blow up. We won't put you in a situation where you could be badly hurt. I don't think Stardust is the right horse for you."

"But I want to keep her." Ashleigh gripped her father's arm. "Dad, please. I'll move slower with her. I won't even ride her until she's absolutely ready. You have to let me try."

Mrs. Griffen gazed at Stardust, who stood placidly in her stall. "She's calmed right down." She looked at Ashleigh and sighed. "She's so erratic, Ash. Her behavior just doesn't make sense."

"I'll just keep riding her in the paddock," Ashleigh said. "Please don't take her away. You said if I kept my grades up and helped Rory, I could keep her."

"We didn't know she was going to be so flighty," Mrs. Griffen said. "There was nothing out there to set her off. You can't enjoy riding a horse that might explode under you at any moment. Besides, it's just not safe."

"It was my fault," Ashleigh cried. "I wasn't paying attention."

Mrs. Griffen looked at Ashleigh and sighed. "You'd have more fun on a horse you could relax on," she said.

"But we don't have another horse. We only have Stardust."

"We're sorry, Ashleigh, but we need to put your safety first," Mr. Griffen said. He and Mrs. Griffen walked away, neither of them looking very happy.

Ashleigh turned to Stardust. "Why did you have to act so stupid?" she demanded. "We were just starting to have fun together and you blew it for both of us."

"I think it was aluminum foil."

The voice made Ashleigh jump. She spun around to face the stranger who had been talking to Kurt a short while before.

"What?" Ashleigh frowned at the man, who was looking at Stardust. The mare hung her head over the stall door and whuffed at him.

"I said it was tinfoil. That's what spooked your horse." He stroked Stardust's nose gently.

Ashleigh stared at the man. "You saw us, too?"

He nodded. "I was watching you ride up the lane, and then I saw a silver flash on the ground. I'll bet if we walk up there and look, there'll be a bit of foil."

If light reflecting off a piece of foil flashed in Stardust's eyes, no wonder she jumped, Ashleigh thought. "Do you really think so, Mr.—?"

He held out his hand. "Call me Jonas," he said, clasping Ashleigh's hand in a firm handshake. "Now, let's walk up between the paddocks. Shouldn't leave garbage lying around, anyway."

Buoyed by a spark of hope, Ashleigh walked with Jonas up the grassy lane, stopping near the place where she'd fallen. "Right here is where she spooked," she said, pointing at the spot where Stardust's hooves had gouged the earth.

"Look." Jonas pointed at the ground near the fence. Caught against the fence post was a piece of shiny aluminum foil. As they watched, a big gust of wind lifted it, making the foil flutter. It caught the light, and Ashleigh blinked as it sent a sudden flash of blinding light right into her eye.

Jonas picked up the foil and wadded it into a ball. "Hard to say for sure," he said, "but what do you want to bet that's what spooked your horse?"

Ashleigh threw her arms around the man, startling

him. "Thank you," she cried. "You've saved Stardust!" She wheeled around and raced for the house.

Her parents listened closely while Ashleigh told them how Jonas had discovered the cause of Stardust's behavior.

Her father looked thoughtful. Finally her turned to her mother. "Elaine—" he started to say, but she held up her hand.

"Stardust still bolted, Derek," she said.

"I know," Mr. Griffen said. "But if Ashleigh will work with her, she can teach Stardust to control her need to run when she's scared."

"I'll do it," Ashleigh said. "I know I can help her."

"Stardust still may not be the right horse for you, though," her mother said.

"But Dad just said . . ." Ashleigh let her voice trail off. Her parents wouldn't put up with an argument.

"We need to know you're safe on her when you take off for rides with Mona," her father said. "If a little bit of foil spooked her, what would she do if you rode past a mailbox or, worse, if a dog ran at her? She may be fine in the paddock, but you don't want to spend all your time riding in little circles. She needs a lot of work, Ashleigh. Do you think you have the patience to see this through?"

Ashleigh looked from one parent to the other. "I

can do it. Let me show you. Didn't I get my math grade up? Haven't I been working with Rory, just like you asked? I can help Stardust. You have to give us another chance."

Her parents looked at each other, and her mother nodded slowly. "One more chance. If she doesn't get past that kind of behavior fast, we can't keep her, Ashleigh."

Ashleigh stood in front of Stardust's stall later that day. "We're getting another chance, girl. But we need to work hard and show my parents what we can do. You don't want to get sent away, do you?"

Stardust pricked her ears and walked to the stall door, hanging her head over it. She pressed her nose against Ashleigh's chest and chuffed. Ashleigh leaned her cheek against Stardust's perfect white star.

"You do like me, don't you? Don't you want to stay here and go riding with Mona and Frisky?"

Stardust rubbed her head against Ashleigh as she fondled the mare's ears.

"Okay, Stardust. This is it. One last chance for both of us. And we're going to show them, aren't we, girl?"

11

"You two seem to be working things out pretty well."

Ashleigh glanced to where Kurt stood beside the paddock, resting his hands on the rail. She flashed him a quick smile, then turned back to Stardust. When she flapped a shiny red plastic placemat in the mare's face, Stardust snorted but didn't move. Ashleigh set down the placemat and stroked Stardust's nose.

"I hope this is working," she said. "If Stardust keeps flipping out over little things, my parents won't let me keep her. After what she did yesterday, I thought they were going to load her up right away."

Kurt settled his gaze on the mare, looking thoughtful. "I think you're doing great," he said.

Stardust stood quietly, waiting for Ashleigh's next cue. Ashleigh wished she felt more sure of Stardust, but in spite of the horse's calmness just then, all

145

Ashleigh could think of was how suddenly Stardust could move when she panicked.

"I'm going to Hopewell this afternoon to say goodbye to Kira. She's going home today. Do you want to go along?"

"Today!" Ashleigh gasped. Kira. With everything that had happened with Stardust, she had completely forgotten her friend. "Of course I want to see her," she added.

"I'll be leaving in about an hour," Kurt told her.

"Okay," Ashleigh said. "I'll tell my parents."

After Kurt left, Ashleigh spent a little while longer trying to help Stardust get used to the strange objects littering the ground near Ashleigh's feet. Besides the placemat, there was a Mylar balloon, an umbrella, a bicycle wheel, a plastic bottle, and Rory's squeaky bathtub duck. After sniffing the objects and looking them over, Stardust settled down and remained calm and quiet. Ashleigh was sure Stardust had more surprises behind those soft brown eyes, but the strange things didn't seem to upset her, no matter what Ashleigh did with them.

Still, after being caught by surprise the day before, Ashleigh didn't know if she could trust the mare outside the paddock. It was one thing to show Stardust a few things in the paddock. It would be a lot different if they were riding along the road and came upon something unexpected.

Ashleigh put Stardust away and hurried up to the house to change her clothes before going to Hopewell. Rory sat on the floor rolling his dump truck back and forth. In the back of the truck, looking as if he owned the world, sat Prince Charming, apparently enjoying the ride.

Ashleigh started to speak, then stopped. Rory wasn't hurting anything, and the cat clearly enjoyed the attention. Rory was mad enough at her for cutting their ride short the day before. She wouldn't complain if he wanted to play with Prince Charming. The kitten seemed to like him almost as much as he liked Ashleigh. At least Prince Charming still slept on her bed. *For now, anyway,* she thought, hurrying through the room.

She found her mother in the den, typing something into the computer. "Can I go to Hopewell with Kurt? Kira's leaving today to go home. She's much better."

Her mother glanced up, a distracted smile on her face. "Well, good for her. Of course you can go," she said, and then she added, "Did Kurt tell you his big news yet?"

Ashleigh shook her head. "No," she said. "What news?"

"I'll let him tell you," her mother said, turning back to the computer.

Ashleigh rushed upstairs and threw on clean clothes, then raced back to the barn, wondering all the while what Kurt's big news could be.

On the ride to the treatment center, Ashleigh waited for Kurt to say something, but he kept quiet. Kurt seemed preoccupied, drumming his fingers on the steering wheel as they drove through the countryside.

When they got to Hopewell, Kira was glowing, surrounded by her friends and the staff at the center. Her suitcases were packed, and her horse posters were rolled into a neat bundle. Ashleigh felt sad, but she was thrilled to see Kira looking so well.

She left the group of well-wishers gathered in the entryway and hurried over to Kurt and Ashleigh. Kira hugged Kurt good-bye, and he squeezed her close. His eyes looked sad, but he was smiling.

"Thanks for everything, Kurt," Kira said, stepping back.

"You take care of yourself, all right?" Kurt said. Then he went off to the staff room to meet Kira's parents.

Kira turned to Ashleigh. "I still can't believe I finally get to go home," she said, excitement shining in her eyes.

"I'm so glad for you," Ashleigh said. "I know I haven't been to see you in a while, but I'm really going to miss you, Kira."

"I'll write," the other girl promised. "And you have to come and check on Lightning once in a while and let me know how she's doing, okay?"

"Of course I will," Ashleigh promised.

Kira grabbed her hand. "Let's go see her before I leave."

They slipped out the door before anyone noticed, and hurried to the barn.

Kira opened the side door, and both girls peeked inside. Barney the goat was curled up in front of Lightning's stall door. Lightning was dozing, her head hung over the door, her nose hovering just above Barney's black and white back. The girls gazed at the contented animals for a second, then Ashleigh spoke Lightning's name.

The horse jerked her head up and whinnied, her eyes fixed on the two girls at the barn door. Barney scrambled to his feet and bleated at them.

Ashleigh led the way to the stall. They passed Ollie the pig, who grunted softly, lying on his side in a deep bed of straw. Mortimer quacked and ruffled his feathers, then settled back down on a bale of straw once he recognized the visitors.

Lightning pressed against the stall door, whuffing and nickering as the girls approached her. Barney ambled off, bleating in a pathetic voice.

Ashleigh and Kira laughed. "I think he's mad that we interrupted his nap," Ashleigh said.

"Oh, Lightning." Kira wrapped her arms around the mare's neck. "I'm going to miss you so much." Lightning snuffled against Kira's chest. A tear trickled down Kira's cheek.

Ashleigh stayed back, letting Kira say good-bye to the mare. At least Lightning was close enough that Ashleigh could visit the horse whenever she had time. It wouldn't be so easy for Kira to come back, Ashleigh realized sympathetically.

When Kira looked over at her and tried to smile, Ashleigh moved close to the stall. As soon as Lightning caught Ashleigh's scent, the mare's head popped up. Her ears sprang forward and she nickered, like a mare to its foal.

"Hi, Lightning," Ashleigh said, putting her hand on the horse's long nose. "You look happy, girl. Do you miss me, or are you just glad to have a visitor?"

The barn door slid open, and Kyle, a blond boy a little older than Rory, rolled his wheelchair inside. "Hi, guys," the six-year-old said. "I just got some carrots from the kitchen for Lightning."

When Kyle rolled up to the stall, Ashleigh moved out of the way. Lightning hung her head low so that Kyle could pet her. He beamed up at Ashleigh and Kira. "I just love her," he said, stroking the mare's forehead. "She likes carrots, don't you, Lightning?"

Ashleigh stepped farther back, but Lightning kept her nose in Kyle's lap.

She glanced at Kira and smiled, then looked back at Kyle and Lightning. Both boy and horse looked content. "You take good care of her, okay, Kyle?" Kira said.

Kyle glanced up at Kira and grinned broadly. "Okay," he said, hugging the mare's head. Lightning nudged him. "Thanks for bringing her to us, Ashleigh," he said, pressing his cheek to Lightning's nose. Kira turned for the door and Ashleigh followed. They left the barn quietly, leaving Kyle and Lightning together.

"Lightning will always have new kids to take care of her," Kira said as she pulled the door shut.

Ashleigh nodded but didn't say anything. She didn't trust her voice. Ashleigh knew, without any doubt, that Lightning was where she belonged.

By the time they returned to the main building, Kira's parents had loaded her suitcases into their car. Kira hesitated by the car door, holding the roll of posters out for Ashleigh. "Will you remember me whenever you look at these?" she asked.

Ashleigh nodded. "Of course I will," she said, giving Kira a big hug. "I'm really going to miss you a lot, but I'm so glad you get to go home."

Ashleigh watched Kira climb into the car, and she waved until it had disappeared down the long, tree-lined drive. She rubbed at her eyes, wiping at the tears clinging to her lashes.

"Ready to go home?"

She glanced up at Kurt and nodded.

They climbed into Kurt's truck, and he started down the road to Edgardale. "It's hard to say good-bye, isn't it?"

Ashleigh stared out the windshield at the clouds gathering in the sky. "Yeah, but Kira's going home. It's good that she's better."

Kurt glanced over at her. "I'm happy for her, too. You know," he went on, "I think it's about time for me to go home as well."

"Home?" Ashleigh was confused. "Kurt, you live in the apartment over the barn. Isn't that home?"

Kurt shook his head. "That's not my home, Ashleigh. I'm talking about going home to Missouri. That's where my sister, Kelly, and her husband live. They've been asking me to come back for months."

"So you want to leave Edgardale?"

"Edgardale is a great place, but it isn't home for me,

Ashleigh. It helped me to work here while I dealt with my own feelings about losing my daughter. And helping the kids at Hopewell has helped me, too. But I can't stay here forever."

"So you're going to leave, and we'll never see you again?"

Kurt lifted his shoulders. "Since I'll be working with Kelly and Mike at Stonecrest, the breeding farm they manage, I might be bringing horses down to Kentucky once in a while. I'll be sure to stop in whenever I get a chance."

"When are you leaving?" Ashleigh was getting tired of saying good-bye. First Lightning, then Kira, and now Kurt.

"This afternoon," Kurt said. "I'm all packed. I didn't have that much to take care of. I'll be heading for Kansas City after I drop you off."

"But what about your job?"

"Your parents and I discussed this several weeks ago, and they hired my replacement today. You met him, too."

Ashleigh remembered the stranger at the barn who'd helped her figure out what had spooked Stardust.

"Jonas?"

"That's him," Kurt said. "Nice man. He knows a lot about horses. He'll take good care of the broodmares."

Ashleigh gazed out the window in silence for a minute. "I wish you could just stay."

"I need to spend time with my family, Ashleigh. I was so upset when my little girl died that I just took off. It's taken me a while, but I've learned you can't run away from things."

Ashleigh looked at Kurt, but she didn't know what to say. She turned to look out the window and remained silent, thinking about everything.

When they pulled into the drive at Edgardale, Kurt drove Ashleigh up to the house. Ashleigh sat in the passenger seat, reluctant to get out and say good-bye.

"What about Rory and Caroline?" Ashleigh asked. "Have you talked to them, too?"

Kurt nodded. "I already said good-bye. I don't want to do it again—it's too hard. And I wanted to save the best for last," he added, giving Ashleigh's shoulder a squeeze. Ashleigh turned and hugged him.

"I'm going to miss you, Kurt."

"Good luck with that new horse, Ashleigh," Kurt said. "And you take care."

"I will," Ashleigh said. She jumped from the car and hurried into the house, pulling her jacket up to her chin as a gust of wind blew rain into her face. The rain was starting to fall harder. Ashleigh turned to wave at Kurt as he drove away.

Caroline met her at the doorway, a panicky look on her face. "Ash, Rory is gone!"

Ashleigh frowned at her sister. What more could happen to her in one day? "Where are Mom and Dad?" she asked. "Their car is gone. Maybe Rory went with them."

"No!" Caroline wrung her hands together. "They had to go to Lexington. I was supposed to be watching him."

Ashleigh's jaw dropped. "Did you look in his room?"

"Of course I did," Caroline snapped.

Ashleigh remembered Rory's last hiding place. "Did you check the barn?"

"Of course I did," Caroline said again. "He's not there."

"Did you try the hayloft?" Ashleigh asked, remembering where Rory had gone the last time he went missing.

Caroline's face brightened. "Maybe that's where he went. He couldn't have gone far in this weather. Ash, we have to find him before Mom and Dad get home. Come on." Caroline pulled her coat on and raced out of the house, Ashleigh following close behind.

The barn was quiet except for the sounds of the horses in their stalls. Ashleigh and Caroline hurried toward the stairs leading to the hayloft.

"Rory?" Caroline called, but there was no response.

She scrambled up the stairs, yelling her brother's name.

Ashleigh started up after her, then stopped cold when she looked down at the row of stalls.

"Caro," she yelled. "Get down here, quick!"

"Just a second," her sister called back. Caroline appeared at the top of the stairs and looked down at Ashleigh, frowning. "He's not up here," she said, starting down.

Ashleigh shook her head and pointed silently at the stalls. Moe's stall door hung open, and the pony was nowhere in sight.

Caroline looked, and her jaw went slack. "Oh, no," she moaned. "He let Moe go! No wonder he's hiding."

Ashleigh dashed down the stairs and into the tack room, a sick feeling in the pit of her stomach. She stared at the empty rack where Moe's saddle usually sat. She hurried back to Caroline, her face pale. "Moe's saddle is gone," she said.

Overhead the rain pounded on the barn roof, and a gust of wind blasted down the aisle from the open door. "Rory didn't let Moe go. He's out riding him. Oh, Caro," she whispered, staring at her sister in horror. "They're somewhere out there in this storm!"

12

"What do we do?" Caroline's words came out in a terrified whisper. "He could be anywhere."

"How long has he been gone?" Ashleigh stared out the open barn door toward the lane leading to the woods.

"I don't know," Caroline moaned. "I got a phone call, and when I hung up he was gone."

Ashleigh wanted to scream. Caroline spent hours at a time blabbing on the phone. Rory could have left hours earlier and she wouldn't have noticed. Ashleigh started to snap at her sister for being so irresponsible, then caught herself.

If Ashleigh hadn't cut Rory's ride short that weekend, he probably wouldn't have gotten so upset and run off. If Ashleigh had just climbed back on Stardust, they could have continued on the ride. Rory was angry with her, and Ashleigh was at least as responsible for Rory's running away as Caroline was. She clamped her mouth shut. The important thing was to find their little brother.

She stared out the door at the woods. The tops of the distant trees whipped back and forth in the wind. Had Rory headed for the trails that wound through the woods behind Edgardale on his own? She thought he probably had, intending to finish the ride that had been cut short when Stardust spooked and tossed Ashleigh off. But he had never been on those trails on his own.

Her stomach dropped as she remembered the trail ride she and Mona had gone on, riding Moe and Silver. That ride had taken them miles and miles from Edgardale, to the farm where they found Lightning and her abusive owner. The whole experience had been scary for her and Mona, and they were twice as old as Rory.

"Don't just stand there, Ash. Let's go!" Caroline tugged at the sleeve of Ashleigh's jacket.

Ashleigh jerked her arm away. "Go get Stardust's saddle," she said, wheeling around to face her sister. Caroline stood looking at her with a blank expression.

"Now!" Ashleigh darted toward the mare's stall. Stardust had her head hanging over the stall door, looking expectantly at Ashleigh.

If she was going to find Rory and Moe, Ashleigh had to get on the trails. But if Stardust acted up, Ashleigh could very well end up on the ground again, of no use to Rory at all.

For a moment she wavered. She and Caroline could go after Rory on foot. It would take longer, but if they kept calling, they might hear Moe whinny, or Rory might find them.

But that could take hours. Stardust bobbed her head at Ashleigh as if to say, *Let's go.* Ashleigh inhaled deeply and quickly swung the stall door open. She didn't have time to be afraid. Rory needed her help.

Ashleigh wasted no time leading Stardust from her stall. They met Caroline halfway to the tack room. Ashleigh shoved the lead rope into Caroline's hand and grabbed the saddle, quickly settling it on Stardust's back.

"What are you going to do with her?" Caroline stamped her foot. "We need to get help and find Rory. She's just going to give you more trouble, Ash."

Ashleigh didn't bother looking up as she hastily tightened the girth. "I know he's in the woods. We'll never find him on foot. Stardust and I can get there a lot faster." She straightened and snatched the lead rope from Caroline.

"I'll get her bridle," Caroline said, hurrying off.

Ashleigh led Stardust to the tack room door as Caroline ducked in and emerged a moment later with Stardust's bridle and Ashleigh's riding helmet.

"Call the Gardeners and tell them Rory went into the woods on Moe," Ashleigh said as she slipped the bridle on over Stardust's halter and led the mare toward the barn door. "And I'm going after them," she added determinedly.

"Be careful," Caroline warned, and raced to the barn office to use the phone.

Ashleigh fastened the chin strap on her helmet. "We have to find Rory before it gets dark, girl. You have to be good for me. You just have to."

Ashleigh led Stardust out of the barn. As soon as the rain began pelting Stardust's coat, the mare snorted and shied. Ashleigh kept a grip on the reins, bringing the mare's head around. She hesitated, trying to settle the trembling in her knees. What if Stardust sent her flying before they even left the stable yard?

"Stardust, you *have* to be good. Please." The mare cocked one ear toward Ashleigh and let out a long, whistling breath. Ashleigh took a deep breath herself, then swung up onto Stardust's back. To her relief Stardust stood still, waiting for a cue.

Ashleigh slipped her feet into the stirrups, gathered

up her reins, and peered through the pouring rain at the trees. Somewhere under that dark canopy her little brother was lost and frightened. She couldn't waste time being scared for herself. Ashleigh picked up the reins and urged Stardust into a trot. Stardust moved quickly, heading down the lane toward the dark stand of trees at the edge of the Griffens' farm.

Ashleigh felt her hands tremble, and she pressed her fists against the mare's neck. *Knock it off,* she ordered herself. *Think of how scared Rory must be, lost in the woods.* The downpour grew heavier, and Ashleigh shivered in her wet jacket. She hoped Rory was wearing something waterproof. She sat straight in the saddle and forced herself to focus on rescuing her brother.

As they approached the spot where Stardust had spooked earlier, Ashleigh couldn't help but tense up. What if Stardust remembered the foil? Even though it wasn't there, she might jump anyway. Ashleigh braced herself, ready for anything, but Stardust kept trotting forward, her ears alert and her pace steady. Ashleigh breathed a sigh of relief.

"Good girl," she murmured, patting the mare's neck. Feeling more confident, she leaned forward and squeezed, urging the mare into a canter. Stardust picked up her pace, and her canter felt wonderful to

Ashleigh, like floating on air. Still, this was no pleasure ride, and it felt as though they were moving too slowly. After a few seconds Ashleigh pushed Stardust into a gallop. The rain whipped in her face, and Ashleigh had to keep sweeping the water from her eyes. But Stardust kept moving forward toward the trees.

Ashleigh wished she were riding for fun. She wanted to savor the feeling of being on Stardust's back while the mare covered the ground with long, smooth strides. Instead Ashleigh kept her eyes ahead, searching for any sign of Moe and Rory. When they neared the woods she slowed Stardust to a walk, pausing to look at the soft ground under the trees. A clear set of small hoofprints led onto one trail.

Ashleigh didn't have time to stop and think. Her little brother was somewhere in the woods. She urged Stardust forward. Stardust snorted and danced around, fighting to stay clear of the trees.

Ashleigh petted the mare's neck. "You have to trust me," she said in a soothing voice. "I've been in here hundreds of times. You'll be safe, Stardust. Honest."

Stardust flicked her ears back, listening to Ashleigh's calm voice, then stepped forward in response to Ashleigh's urging. They moved onto the narrow trail. Ashleigh ducked to miss a branch. She didn't remember the trail being so cramped. Riding through here on the ponies was a lot different from being on a horse. A wet bough slapped her shoulder, and Ashleigh grabbed at Stardust's mane to keep her balance.

The trail grew even narrower, and Stardust jumped when a tree branch brushed her side. Ashleigh automatically tightened her legs on the mare's sides and pulled on the reins.

"It isn't a whip," Ashleigh said, trying to keep her voice from shaking. She released Stardust's head and nudged her forward again. "Please, Stardust, don't spook on me now. Rory needs us."

They seemed to wind forever along the shadowy path. At least the rain wasn't as heavy under the thick canopy of trees. Ashleigh shivered as the cold seeped through her wet clothes.

Suddenly Stardust stopped dead. "Keep going," Ashleigh said, pressing her heels to the mare's sides and trying to keep her panic at bay. Instead Stardust arched her neck and released a whinny that made Ashleigh jiggle in the saddle.

When she heard Moe's answering whinny, Ashleigh wanted to cry with relief. "Rory!" she yelled. "Where are you?"

"Over here!" Stardust followed the trail willingly now, and soon they found Rory and Moe standing under a big tree. The pony looked as calm and patient as ever, while Rory looked frightened and miserable on his back.

"I got lost," Rory said. "I thought Moe would take me home if I let him go, but instead he just stopped under this stupid tree and wouldn't move." He swiped at his face. With all the rain falling, Ashleigh wasn't sure how much of the wetness on his cheeks was rain and how much was teardrops.

Ashleigh jumped from the saddle and rushed to where her brother sat on Moe. "We were so worried about you. Never disappear like that again!"

Rory leaned against Moe's wet, fuzzy neck. "Will you take me home, Ash? I'm tired of sitting here."

Ashleigh patted Moe's neck. "Good old Moe. He knew it was starting to rain and he didn't want to get wet. Come on, pony." She took Moe's reins and led him to Stardust's side. The mare eyed Moe suspiciously, but she didn't strike out. Ashleigh mounted up and, with Rory and Moe in tow, led the way down the path toward the farm.

By the time they reached the barn, the rain had lessened. The barn lights were on and Mr. and Mrs. Griffen stood in the stable yard with Caroline, watching anxiously.

"Thank goodness!" Mrs. Griffen wrapped her arms around Rory and lifted him from Moe's saddle. "You had everyone worried sick. Caroline," she said, "please call the Gardeners and let them know everything is fine now."

Caroline hurried off. Mrs. Griffen hugged Rory close. "Let's get you inside and dried off," she said, unbuckling his helmet.

"Thanks, Ash. I'm glad you and Stardust came looking for me," Rory called as Mrs. Griffen led him up the house.

"Me too," Ashleigh called back.

Mr. Griffen took Moe's reins from Ashleigh. "I'll take care of the horses, Ash. You can go up with your mom and Rory. You need to get dry, too. We don't want you getting sick."

Ashleigh jumped from Stardust's back but held on to the reins. "That's all right, Dad. I can take care of her myself. She is my responsibility, after all."

Mr. Griffen looked from Ashleigh to the mare and shrugged. "Well, if you're not too tired, Ashleigh," he said, shaking his head and smiling as he led Moe away.

Ashleigh brought Stardust into the barn and put her in crossties. She pulled the saddle from the mare's back and started toward the tack room. Just then Caroline came out of the office and reached out to take the saddle from her.

"I'll oil this for you, Ash." She pulled off her warm coat. "Give me your jacket and put this on."

"But I'm going to clean Stardust up. You don't want horsehair and dirt on your nice coat," Ashleigh protested.

Caroline shook her head. "It's only a coat, Ash. I can wash it. You're soaked. I don't want you to be cold."

Ashleigh peeled off her wet jacket and slipped her arms into the sleeves of Caroline's coat. The warm fabric felt good on her cold skin.

Since Caroline was taking care of her tack, Ashleigh took extra time rubbing Stardust down with a big, fluffy towel. The mare relaxed her head, stretching out her neck and closing her eyes with pleasure.

"You were great, Stardust," Ashleigh murmured as she rubbed the mare's strong, sloping shoulder. Stardust pricked her ears and turned her head toward Ashleigh at the sound of her voice. The mare gazed at Ashleigh with a gentle, inquisitive expression. Then Ashleigh realized that Stardust had gone well for her because she had understood what Ashleigh wanted. Stardust wanted to please her because she loved Ashleigh, and Ashleigh loved Stardust, too. It had happened. Stardust was *hers*.

Ashleigh knew her parents might not see things the

same way. She would just have to wait and see what the verdict would be.

Ashleigh mixed a warm bran mash for Stardust and Moe and then trudged up to the house, tired and cold. She wasn't in any hurry, though. Her parents were going to tell her that Rory's going off had been as much her fault as Caroline's. They had made it very clear that part of keeping Stardust for her to ride depended on her working with Rory and Moe. Ashleigh had been cutting their rides short so that she could spend more time with Stardust. That wasn't fair to Rory, and she knew it.

Mrs. Griffen met her at the kitchen door. Ashleigh was waiting for some sort of scolding, but to her surprise, her mother hugged her.

"You go up and take a hot shower. I'll have hot chocolate ready when you come down," she said.

"Are you still thinking of taking Stardust away from me?" Ashleigh asked worriedly, looking from her mother to where her father stood in the kitchen. The sooner they got this over with, the better.

"Well, that was a brave thing you did out there, Ashleigh. Reckless, but brave," her father said, looking thoughtful. *Maybe they aren't mad at me after all*, Ashleigh thought.

"So . . . ?" she pressed.

"We'll discuss it later," her father said vaguely.

Ashleigh started to protest, but Ashleigh's father gave her a warning look, so she pressed her mouth shut and stomped up the stairs.

After her shower, Ashleigh put on her pajamas. It felt good to be clean and warm. She padded down the stairs and peeked into the living room. Rory was lying on the sofa, Prince Charming curled up on his stomach.

Ashleigh crossed the room to look down at her brother. "Rory, you really have to quit running away. You scared me half to death."

"I wasn't running away," Rory said, squirming into a sitting position. "I wanted to go on a real ride, but you didn't want to. You used to ride Moe all over the place. I thought he could just take me. He's been through the woods lots of times." Rory started to cry. "I'm sorry, Ash."

Ashleigh sat beside her brother. Prince Charming purred loudly, snuggling in between them. "I'm sorry we didn't go on much of a ride yesterday, Rory. But from now on, things are going to be different. We're going to have some great rides with Stardust and Moe."

Ashleigh glanced up to see her parents standing in the doorway.

It was all or nothing. She decided to risk it.

"Do I get to keep Stardust? Can she be *my* horse?" Ashleigh asked, and held her breath, waiting for her parents' response.

The Griffens looked at each other, silently conferring.

Then her father nodded, breaking into a grin. Ashleigh jumped to her feet. "Thank you!" she shouted happily. "You'll see. Stardust is going to be the best horse in the world!"

Ashleigh darted around her parents and into the kitchen.

"Ash! Where are you going now?" her mother called.

"Down to the barn," Ashleigh called over her shoulder. "I have to give Stardust a carrot and tell her that she's really mine!"

Dear Diary,

Guess what? I finally have my own horse. Stardust is mine to keep! I'm so happy. I know we still have a lot of problems to work out, but we understand each other now. Soon we'll be galloping through the fields and jumping fences with Mona and Frisky. I can't wait to see what we'll do!

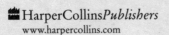